"Enough!

"You are banned from the Continuum while we deliberate on your fate."

That took him aback. "Banned?"

Q gave him the stare she always used when he annoyed her—which was fairly often, if it came to that—and said, "You're the one who enjoys flitting about the cosmos spreading chaos in your wake, dear. So go do it."

And then he was gone from the Continuum. Aghast, he tried to access it, but failed. He changed into a star-singer, which worked just fine. Then he turned into an Aldebaran serpent, a Belzoidian flea, a Traveler, and a baseball bat.

I still have my powers. I've simply been denied the ability to go home.

He considered his next move. The Continuum could take ages to deliberate, and he wasn't sure the universe had that long. Even if it did, he was hardly about to wait around.

I may as well drop in on Jean-Luc. Make him an offer he can't refuse.

STAR TREK
THE NEXT GENERATION®

Q&A

KEITH R.A. DeCANDIDO

*Based on Star Trek: The Next Generation
created by Gene Roddenberry*

POCKET BOOKS
New York   London   Toronto   Sydney

Pocket Books
A Division of Simon & Schuster, Inc.
1230 Avenue of the Americas
New York, NY 10020

This book is a work of fiction. Names, characters, places and incidents either are products of the author's imagination or are used fictitiously. Any resemblance to actual events or locales or persons, living or dead, is entirely coincidental.

This book is published by Pocket Books, a division of Simon & Schuster, Inc., under exclusive license from CBS Studios Inc.

First Pocket Books paperback edition October 2007

POCKET and colophon are registered trademarks of Simon & Schuster, Inc.

For information about special discounts for bulk purchases, please contact Simon & Schuster Special Sales at 1-800-456-6798 or business@simonandschuster.com.

Cover art and design by Jae Song

Manufactured in the United States of America

10   9   8   7   6   5   4   3   2   1

ISBN-13:   978-1-4165-2741-1
ISBN-10:   1-4165-2741-9

To John de Lancie,
whose magnificent performances
made this book possible

HISTORIAN'S NOTE

The main events in this book take place during the decline of the Romulan Empire brought about by the rise of Shinzon (*Star Trek Nemesis*). The *Enterprise* has been refitted for space, and Captain Jean-Luc Picard has filled her ranks with some new and some old faces. The captain awaits Starfleet's ruling on his refusing to obey orders during the most recent Borg incursion (*Star Trek: The Next Generation—Resistance*).

FIRST PROLOGUE

SOMEWHERE . . .

THEY HELD OFF ON LETTING THIS UNIVERSE DIE IN the hopes that it would provide something interesting. They slowed entropy to a crawl, preventing chaos from overwhelming all and sundry, and then They waited for someone to make it through.

Several races found the world but either were not blessed with sufficient understanding to navigate the hazards and think their way through the defenses or simply missed them altogether.

Finally, someone made it through. Not only did this race achieve all the goals, but they also prepared an elaborate presentation, showing how advanced they were, the breakthroughs they'd made, the lessons they'd learned. It took quite some time and was incredibly thorough, filled with re-creations using a variety of types of technology that They had mastered over the millennia.

It bored Them to tears. So They let the universe

die, hoping the *next* one would be more interesting.

It was, as it turns out. Eons later when denizens of this next universe discovered Them, and made it through, they showed Them the millions of worlds they'd conquered. Their empire straddled six galaxies, thanks to their ability to travel instantly from one world to another without need of conveyances, and they used that ability to show Them all the worlds they'd brought under their purview.

However, more interesting than deadly dull was still fairly dull, and They let this universe die too.

The representatives of the next universe had achieved enlightenment by evolving into beings of pure energy who spent all their days in contemplation of the great mysteries of the universe. This went beyond boring and into stultifying, and They wiped out that universe with great glee.

The next bunch stumbled across Them by accident and were convinced that they were victims of some kind of put-on. For the amusement value alone, They almost let that one live, but they were too pathetic to be worth saving.

Nobody, it seemed to Them, got it.

Maybe the next universe . . .

SECOND PROLOGUE

———◆———

SOMEWHERE ELSE . . .

HE WASN'T SURE, OF COURSE. FOR ALL HE AND THE others carried on about their omnipotence, that didn't mean they were omniscient. It was a conundrum that vexed many of them, though he himself never let it bother him all that much. He was too busy having fun—certainly more than the rest of them were.

But it was on one of his jaunts searching for a good time that he found something he hadn't even realized he was looking for.

The species was one of many collections of mortals that infested the universe, and far from the most interesting. They were lodged in an arm of one of the more homogenous galaxies, scurrying about in crude vehicles, trusting tools to accomplish what they were too impatient to let evolution develop on its own. Such impatient peoples tended to burn bright and die young, but this batch had done only the former.

They called themselves humans.

He wasn't the first of the higher entities to deal with them. The Organians, Excalbians, and Metrons had all dallied with humans, mostly either to test them or make pronouncements. (Especially the Organians, who were never happier than when they were making pronouncements.) But they had not interfered overmuch in the humans' development.

And why should they? Just another bunch of mortals in a universe that had far too many of them.

But there was always one thing that all of his people had been on the lookout for, something that would change the face of the universe.

They sought the ones.

He had a very good feeling about these humans after his test. The test itself hadn't been more than an entertaining diversion, but as he went along, he saw something in the humans, in particular, their leader. The captain didn't *seem* like much—short even by human standards, a strangely constructed face, and a tendency to declaim that rivaled the Organians—but he saw a quality in Jean-Luc Picard. There was a glimmer of it in the others as well, but in Picard, it shone like a beacon.

Picard may very well be the one, he thought.

So he went home after toying with them at Deneb V and started to plead his case to the rest of the Q Continuum.

His best advocates, unfortunately, were gone. First of all, there was the philosopher, who was trapped in a comet and had been for the past several moments. His counsel would have been useful. And then there were Q and Q, who had already encountered humanity and were so taken with them that they took their form and went to live with them on their dreary little homeworld, even going so far as to reproduce while in that form (a concept that made him shudder to the very core of his being). They had broken the rules, used their powers while remaining human. Those who tried to straddle both worlds inevitably failed at both.

Sadly, his fellows didn't learn that lesson. After he explained about the humans and their potential to all the other Q, Q looked down on him and said, "If you really believe they are the ones, then the decision is obvious: give one of these humans our power and explain it to them."

He sighed. "That won't *work*. The one *cannot* be a higher form. You *know* They won't accept that."

Q raised one of his eyebrows. "We do not *know* if these humans are the ones. Make this Picard into a Q, and we *will* know."

Shaking his head, he said, "No, that's too risky. I'll make his second, Riker." He smiled. "He's *much* more entertaining."

Rolling her eyes, another Q said, "This isn't about your entertainment, Q."

"Q just said we don't even know, so I might as well have some fun while I'm at it."

Letting out a tired sigh, the first Q said, "Very well, do as you will. But do as we say also, Q. This is too important to bungle."

He bit back a retort—the fact was, nobody believed him. Nobody ever believed him or took him seriously. Not that he gave them reason to—there were any number of youthful indiscretions of his they could throw in his face if they so desired, especially that rather embarrassing business with the Tkon Empire—but even he knew how important it was to find the ones.

So off he went, back to the *U.S.S. Enterprise*, NCC-1701-D, to give William Riker the power of the Q—and see what happened.

1

U.S.S. Enterprise NCC-1701-E
En route to Gorsach IX

Two days before the end of the universe

BEVERLY CRUSHER DABBED SOME ICOBERRY JAM
on her croissant and stared at her breakfast companion. "What are you thinking, Jean-Luc?"

Jean-Luc Picard smiled warmly at her. That alone was a rare gift. Beverly had known Jean-Luc for more years than she was willing to admit to out loud, and the number of times she'd seen that particular smile was few. The number of times she saw it when there was anyone other than the two of them in the room was close to zero.

He sipped from his ceramic cup of Earl Grey tea

before answering the question. "Merely contemplating our current assignment. It's something of a relief actually to be engaged in our mission statement for a change."

"How soon before we arrive at the Gorsach system?" Beverly asked after swallowing a bite of croissant and self-consciously brushing the flakes off her lap.

"We should arrive by tomorrow morning. There'll be a senior staff meeting this afternoon at seventeen thirty."

Beverly nodded. "I'll be spending most of the day doing physicals on the new arrivals."

Jean-Luc set down his teacup on the end table next to the bed, then reached over to cup Beverly's cheek with his right hand. "I must say, Beverly, I prefer this method of eating breakfast."

Reaching over to the tray that sat between them on the bed, Beverly grabbed another croissant and stuck it in his mouth. "You're just saying that because you don't have to clean the bed."

Talking with his mouth full—another sight only Beverly got to see—Jean-Luc said, "I would think that even if I had to clean every crumb myself."

"You're such a romantic." She grabbed the back of his hand and pulled it off her cheek so she could kiss his palm. "Why didn't we do this years ago?" she whispered.

"Because we're both fools. Because . . ." Jean-Luc hesitated. "There were times when I looked at you and still saw my best friend's wife."

Once, that might have angered Beverly, or irked her at the very least. But Jack Crusher had been dead for a long time, and Beverly had seen so many people die or move on—from her son becoming a being on a higher plane of existence to Data's death late last year—that the idea of clinging to Jack's memory seemed foolish now. "I know, Jean-Luc," she said gently. "But there's room in my heart for both of you."

With that, she pulled his head toward hers and they kissed.

They stopped only when the clang of flatware falling to the floor startled both of them. Peering over the side of the bed, Beverly saw that the croissant tray and the jam had upended onto the carpet.

She looked at Jean-Luc and grinned. "Oops."

"Oops, indeed. Suddenly, I'm rather grateful I *don't* have to clean the room myself. Thank heaven for automated janitorial systems."

Beverly chuckled, then she blinked. "Computer, time?"

"The time is zero-seven forty-five hours."

Letting out a long breath, Beverly turned to Jean-Luc. "I'm supposed to be meeting Miranda in fifteen minutes, and you're due on the bridge."

Now Jean-Luc's smile was mischievous, an even bigger rarity. "I'm sure Commander Kadohata can start her morning workout without you—and I *know* Worf can handle the bridge for a few minutes more."

Waggling a finger, Beverly said, "Now, now, Jean-Luc, you're setting a bad example for your crew.

Think of all the newcomers, and the reputation you and this ship carry. Do you really want to let them think the great Jean-Luc Picard is a slugabed?"

It was Jean-Luc's turn to let out a long breath, and he spoke with mock gravity. "I suppose you're right. Heavy is the burden of command."

"But you wear it well." And she kissed him again before untangling herself from the bedsheets—which had gotten into quite a mess—and clambered out of bed.

Jean-Luc also got up from the bed—without, to Beverly's annoyance, nearly as much trouble—and said, "I'm glad to see that Commander Kadohata is adjusting well."

"She is, yes," Beverly said as she climbed out of her bedclothes. "And these morning workouts are important to her—she needs to get back into shape after the pregnancy." Beverly smiled. "She's also on the list of physicals. I want to make sure there aren't any postpartum issues."

"A wise precaution," Jean-Luc said as he did likewise. "Her expertise will be invaluable at Gorsach. I'm sure she'll make a fine second officer."

Beverly nodded as she put on her workout leotard. Lieutenant Commander Miranda Kadohata had been Data's handpicked successor in the role of second officer. She was to take over upon Data's ascension to the role of first officer, following William Riker's moving on to the *Titan* as her new captain. Data's tragic death on the *Scimitar* did nothing to change Miranda's status—but her pregnancy did.

She had hoped to work through to the final weeks, but the twins had other ideas. Miranda had taken maternity leave on Cestus III to have the children at home with her husband and five-year-old daughter.

The twins—Colin and Sylvana—were now doing quite well with Miranda's husband, Vicenzo Farrenga (and, according to Vicenzo, vexing their five-year-old sister, Aoki), and the commander had finally reported to the *Enterprise.*

Miranda was one recent arrival whose presence wasn't due to tragedy. While some of the new faces on the *Enterprise* were taking over for those who had gone with Riker to *Titan,* many were replacements for those killed in action—most recently in a brutal encounter with what Beverly had started thinking of as the new, unimproved Borg. They'd lost seven people, from the conn officer and security chief on down, before the Borg had been stopped.

A mission of exploration was just the thing the crew needed, in Beverly's professional opinion. Beverly still recalled Jean-Luc's complaint during their mission to Evora during the Dominion War: "Can anyone remember when we used to be explorers?"

She looked over at the captain, who was now fully dressed in his uniform. The warm smile was gone. It was as if the uniform came with a force field made of dignity. He seemed to grow half a meter in height and carry himself in a much-less-relaxed manner than he had in bed a few moments ago.

After sliding thick socks up over her ankles, she

walked over to Jean-Luc and put her arms on his shoulders. "I love you, Jean-Luc."

The force field fell for an instant, and he whispered, "I love you, Beverly."

Moments later, they walked out of their shared quarters together, and both of their force fields were back up in full. In their quarters they were Jean-Luc and Beverly, but out here they were the CO and the CMO.

Which is as it should be, she thought. *I get the best of him, the part of him no one else sees. And I couldn't be happier.*

They entered the turbolift. He said, "Bridge," she said, "Deck five." The lift stopped at deck five first, naturally, and she gave Picard a quick nod as she departed.

As the doctor sauntered down the corridor, she tapped her combadge, which was currently attached to the purple silk sash—a gift from Jean-Luc—around her waist. "Crusher to sickbay."

The cheery voice of her Denobulan deputy chief medical officer replied. *"Sickbay, this is Doctor Tropp."* Tropp had stayed on board even after Beverly's temporary departure to head up Starfleet Medical, before she decided to return to the *Enterprise.* Tropp did not yet have the requisite experience to be made CMO in Beverly's place, but he had remained behind to be the assistant to whoever replaced Beverly. She was grateful to have the familiar face, especially since most of the medical staff had transferred—some, like head nurse Alyssa Ogawa, to *Titan.*

"Anything I need to know about?" Beverly asked.

"Just the usual scrapes and bruises. Ensign La Monica came in last night with a fractured arm."

Beverly let out a long breath. "She tried the sky-diving program again, didn't she?"

"Actually, no. Your warnings last time were sufficiently dire that she decided to spend her off-duty time in the Hoobishan Baths."

"I'm almost afraid to ask."

"She slipped on a wet bit of tile and is currently sitting on the biobed swearing never to go near the holodeck as long as she lives."

Chuckling, Beverly said, "That's probably her best move. Anything else?"

"Nothing of consequence. I've been showing Nurse Mimouni some of our trauma procedures."

"Good." Mimouni was a new arrival, fresh out of Starfleet Medical. What Tropp lacked in experience he more than made up for in teaching ability. He was the right person to show her the ropes. "I'll be in the gym for the next hour or so if you need me."

"Acknowledged. Tropp out."

Beverly turned a corner and approached the large gymnasium doors, which were of the wide, hexagon-shaped design that was also used for holodecks and cargo bays. They rolled open to the sound of over two dozen people shouting in unison.

The shouts were rhythmic and alternated with one voice counting. Looking at the far end of the gym to her right, Beverly saw about two dozen people dressed in white gis lined up in three rows, throwing punches to the midsection of an imaginary opponent in front of them. The shouts came on the third punch.

Facing the shouters, and with his back to Beverly, was the broad-shouldered form and prematurely balding head of Lieutenant Zelik Leybenzon, the *Enterprise*'s new chief of security. He was the one doing the counting.

Glancing to her left, Beverly saw that the area that she and Miranda had reserved was empty, which meant Beverly was the first to arrive. She decided to pause and watch the new security chief in action.

Most of Leybenzon's students were wearing white belts with their gis. There were a few exceptions: Stolovitzky and Kapsis both had brown belts, and de Lange had a green one. Leybenzon's belt was black, which even Beverly, with her limited knowledge of the subject, knew indicated a master.

What Beverly did know about martial arts related mostly to the injuries people tended to incur while practicing them. Worf's recent return to the ship had meant a resumption of his *Mok'bara* classes and a concomitant rise in muscle strains and tears, bone bruises, and the occasional fracture, and it looked like Leybenzon was getting into the act as well.

When Leybenzon reached thirty, he stopped counting. Each of the students—who, Beverly realized, were all members of the security detail—stood stock-still, left arm extended from the final punch.

"Reset," Leybenzon then said, and they all crossed their arms in front of their faces while pulling their right foot in toward their left. After half a second, they lowered their arms below their belt and settled into a stance that looked a lot like the traditional military "at ease" pose.

"Front-leaning stance, downward parry," Leybenzon said. "Go!"

At that, all the students stepped back with their right foot and used their left arm to parry downward, their right arm pulling in so their fist was at their right hip. All stood in what Beverly assumed to be the front-leaning stance Leybenzon had called for: left leg bent, knee directly over foot, with the right leg unbent and at an angle. It didn't look especially comfortable to Beverly, but it was a stance that would build strength in the leg muscles.

Leybenzon was pacing now. Sweat gleamed on his high forehead, his close-cropped brown hair having receded almost to the top of his crown. His hazel eyes peered out at the security personnel past a bulbous nose that sat over a thick mustache. "Step in," Leybenzon said. "Downward parry, middle inside block, middle outside block, upper block, then middle inside block/downward parry twice. One!"

All of them angled the front foot, then stepped forward so they were in the same front-leaning stance, but with the right foot forward. They each did a sequence of blocks that Beverly assumed corresponded to the five blocks Leybenzon called out. While they all did the initial downward parry in relative unison, they were not simultaneous in their execution of this combination. Stolovitzky, Kapsis, and de Lange were ahead of the others, perhaps not surprisingly, and Campagna, Balidemaj, and Chao were keeping up fairly well. Others were lagging behind, and some—particularly those in the back row—weren't executing the blocks properly.

"Two!"

They did it again. Two in the back row utterly lost it, finally just giving up and setting their hands in position for the last of the blocks so they were ready for the next set.

"Faster! Three!"

By now they were close to the middle of the floor, only a few meters from where Beverly was standing. She moved back a bit to play it safe.

"Four!" After a second, and before most of them were done, "Five, finish!"

Leybenzon shook his head. "Pathetic. If you had been with me at Chin'toka, we would have lost the planet *again*. Okay. Turn around!"

They each set up for the downward parry again, twisted around, and did the parry with their backs to Beverly.

This time Leybenzon went from one to five much faster. The entire back row—front row, now—was struggling.

Shaking his head some more, Leybenzon said, "Reset."

Again, they all went to the "at ease" position, facing forward.

"I see the next few months will be difficult. These are simple combinations, ones that children can do. I am shuddering at what might happen if we have to enter combat. Okay. Down stomach!"

They all fell to the floor on their stomachs, ready to do push-ups.

"Thirty push-ups," Leybenzon said. "Begin."

Beverly took this opportunity to approach the security chief. "Excuse me, Lieutenant?"

"Now is not a good time," Leybenzon said without even turning to look at Beverly. He walked toward the back row and pushed down on the shoulders of one of the people who'd been struggling with the combinations—Beverly was pretty sure it was Vogel.

"I don't think we've been properly introduced, *Lieutenant,*" Beverly said frostily. "My name is *Commander* Beverly Crusher, the chief medical officer."

Leybenzon's head shot up, and he stared at her for a second. Then he let up on Vogel and stood up straight. "Okay. My apologies, Doctor. What can I do for you?"

"This will only take a second. You were scheduled for a routine physical the day you reported on board. That physical has been rescheduled three times. If you miss the next one, I'm going to be forced to take you off duty." She let out a breath. "It's a routine procedure, Lieutenant, it's nothing to be afraid of."

"I am not afraid, Doctor, I have simply been very

busy." He smirked and indicated the students—some of whom had finished their thirty push-ups and were now hovering above the ground, hands or fists on the floor—with his hands. "As you can see, I have my work cut out for me."

Beverly approached Leybenzon, standing close enough to smell his sweat. He was half a head taller than her, so she looked up right into his eyes. "Physicals are a Starfleet regulation, Lieutenant. And if you don't have yours, you aren't fit for duty."

Vogel was about to do a push-up when Leybenzon literally jumped on his back, knees bent and digging into the ensign's shoulders, shins resting on either side of his spine. "No, this young man is not fit for duty. But I will be changing that. And I promise, Doctor, that I will follow Starfleet regulations."

The doors parted. Beverly looked behind her to see Miranda Kadohata entering with a sheepish expression on her face.

Turning back to Leybenzon, Beverly said, "Good. Enjoy the rest of your class, Lieutenant."

"Yes, sir." Looking down at Vogel, he said, "Push up, Ensign!" while Vogel struggled to do just that.

Beverly sighed as she walked over to join Miranda at the other half of the gym. She shouldn't have been surprised that Zelik Leybenzon didn't take to the formalities very well. He was a mustang, having risen through the ranks during the Dominion War. He had served as a noncommissioned security guard. At the start of the Dominion War, he was posted to the *U.S.S. Andromeda*. His quick thinking in repairing a phaser bank that had been declared "totally nonfunctional" by both the chief engineer and chief of security earned him a battle-field commission.

In the six and a half years since then, he'd worked his way up to lieutenant despite never having done any time at the Academy. After the *Andromeda* he was posted to the ground forces holding Chin'toka, followed by postwar billets on the *Roosevelt* and at Starbase 23.

After the death of Lio Battaglia at the hands of the Borg, Picard had accepted Worf's recommendation of Leybenzon as a new security chief. At first, Beverly had assumed them to be childhood friends— Leybenzon, like Worf, grew up on the farming world of Gault—but Worf and his family had moved to Earth when Leybenzon was still a baby. It turned out that the Klingon had encountered the lieutenant during the Dominion War, when Worf was posted to Deep Space 9, and Leybenzon had left a good impression.

"Sorry I'm late," Miranda said. She spoke with a British accent, even though she was born and raised on Cestus III. "I was chatting with Vicenzo and I simply lost track of time."

Beverly smiled. "Perfectly understandable. How are the twins?"

"Colin can't keep his food down, but the pediatrician refuses to be concerned unless it lasts more than twenty-four hours. Sylvana, on the other hand, tends to wake up and cry at the most inconvenient moments."

"Which makes her a completely normal baby," Beverly said, remembering plenty of sleepless nights when Wesley was an infant. "Sounds to me like they're doing fine. And that's a professional opinion."

"Good to know," Miranda said with a small chuckle.

Settling herself down on the floor, Beverly spread her legs. Miranda did likewise, facing her, pressing her heels into Beverly's ankles to spread the legs farther. After a few minutes, they'd switch positions.

Miranda's jet-black hair was tied into a ponytail, her bangs framing a face that showed her mixed ancestry: Asian eyes above sculpted European cheekbones. Those cheekbones weren't as visible as they were in the picture in her service record, as she was still a bit puffy from the pregnancy.

With Deanna Troi's departure, Beverly had been hoping to find a new morning workout partner and was glad to see that her need for a partner dovetailed nicely with Miranda's desire to regain her body shape. "Aoki wasn't this bad," she had said. "After she was born, I snapped right back to my old weight, but the twins were a trifle more demanding."

Beverly's leotard was green and silver; Miranda had gone for all black with a bright red sash around the waist. On one end of the sash was a stylized seagull with an odd-shaped wooden stick in its mouth—a baseball bat, Miranda had explained. The symbol was the logo of the Port Shangri-La Seagulls, a team in the Cestus Baseball League for which Miranda's sister Olwyn was the starting shortstop.

As Beverly bent over her left leg and grabbed her left foot, Miranda grabbed the doctor's silk sash and used it to anchor Beverly and pull her farther down. "How's Aoki handling things?" Beverly asked as she stretched her groin muscles as far as they would go, then stretched them some more.

"According to Vicenzo, she's now decided the whole thing's a jolly game and that she'll win some sort of prize if she takes good care of the twins." Miranda smiled wryly, even as Beverly straightened and bent toward her right leg. "It can't last, but Vicenzo intends to enjoy it while he can."

"Wise man, your husband."

"Mm. Part of me wishes I was there to help him—and be with the twins, they're so beautiful—but I could hardly pass this opportunity up, could I?"

Nodding acknowledgment, Beverly leaned forward, Miranda leaning back and pulling on the sash. She hadn't yet met Vicenzo Farrenga, but it seemed Miranda was happy with him. She remembered back on the *Enterprise*-D, Miranda had a succession of bad relationships, so when she'd settled down with a linguistics professor at Bacco University back home, Beverly had been thrilled.

Miranda continued, "Second officer of the *Enter-*

prise is the position of a lifetime. That wasn't going to come along twice."

"Probably not, no," Beverly said through sharp breaths as she stretched downward.

Then Beverly straightened, and Miranda let go of the sash. They shifted their feet so that now Beverly's heels pushed on Miranda's ankles. "You were lucky," Miranda said between short breaths as she tried to reach her right foot. "When you were raising Wes, they allowed families on ships."

"They still do, to some extent," Beverly said. While the *Enterprise*-E did not accommodate the familial needs of large numbers of its complement the way the *Enterprise*-D did, families weren't completely forbidden, either. This was in keeping with Starfleet policy in the wake of the arrival of the Borg and later the Dominion. While there were decided advantages to not separating officers and crew from their families for extended periods, there were concomitant disadvantages to having children and civilians on a starship that faced dangers both predictable and unexpected on what seemed like a weekly basis.

Still, exceptions were made. Beverly's departed head nurse had raised her son Noah on the *Enterprise*-E—and alone, after her husband died in the Dominion War. The eight-year-old Noah was now with Alyssa on *Titan*.

Straightening, Miranda said, "Yes, but I can't ask Vicenzo to come here, can I? What would he *do*? The ship has a linguist, and Vicenzo's specialty is ancient languages, not contemporary ones." She went to her left. "Besides, I don't fancy having my children on a starship. I don't think I could bear to have Aoki or the twins go through what poor Jeremy Aster did."

That caused Beverly to shudder. Previously, Miranda had been a sensor officer reporting to Data, and it was during one of the D's missions that Marla Aster died in an accident on an away mission, leaving her young son, who was with her on the ship, orphaned.

"They'd still go through it if you . . ." Beverly hesitated, then decided to be blunt. "If you died here and they were on Cestus. That's what happened to Wes when Jack died." Beverly was pleased to see that she could so comfortably talk about Jack's death, as it had been an open wound for so long.

"True, but they'd be on Cestus and not here. I've read all the reports about that balderdash with the Borg." Miranda straightened, then leaned forward, Beverly pulling on her Seagulls sash. "No. I want my husband and children safe. Besides," and she cracked a grin as she leaned forward, "Vicenzo got tenure last year. I won't be able to pry him out of the university now."

Beverly returned the grin, having had plenty of experience with academics in her time.

"I must say, Bev," Miranda said as they both got to their feet, "I do like that glow you're carrying about. And it's about bloody time too."

"I beg your pardon?" Beverly tried to make her

tone frosty, but she knew she was doing an inadequate job.

"You and the captain, love. Should've done that *years* ago, you ask me. Back on the D, we had a pool going in the sensor room. Thought for sure I'd won it after Kesprytt."

Both women bent over to touch their toes. Beverly was able to put her palms flat on the floor, while Miranda struggled to get the tips of her fingers to brush the tops of her feet. "Well, thank you for saying I glow," Beverly said tartly. "I wasn't aware of any incandescence, but I'll take your word for it."

"You should."

"To be honest," Beverly said, letting out a long breath as she straightened, "I'm happy. And what's amazing is that I know I'm happy because I've—we've . . ." She sighed again and let her arms fall to her sides. "We came very close a couple of times—then the Federation was swept up into the war—and even before that, the paranoia and the tensions. Starfleet needed combat doctors on the front lines, and I knew where my duty was. I think we started pushing each other away rather than face the possibility of losing each other."

"What changed?" Miranda asked gently. They had given up any pretense of working out. The occasional shouts of the security personnel could be heard from the other side of the gym.

"The head of Starfleet Medical was retiring and wanted me to take over. The war was over, and we'd pushed each other so far away, it didn't look like we would ever be pulled back. Data died, Will and Deanna moved on—it seemed like I should move on too. I thought I could do more on Earth."

"And then?"

For just a moment, Beverly could hear an echo of Deanna in Miranda's voice. She smiled. "A mission to Kevratas, one where I almost got killed, and Jean-Luc and I both realized that we were being ridiculous." She chuckled. "You'd think with Will and Deanna finally tying the knot, one of us would've gotten the hint, but apparently not."

Miranda shrugged. "If there's one thing I learned when Vicenzo and I stumbled across each other, it's that these things happen when they get 'round to happening, and not a second before."

"Where did you two meet?"

Holding up the sash, she said, "At a ball game. Vicenzo's father is the general manager of the Sehlats, so he and I were both in the VIP seats at a PSL/Palombo game." At Beverly's look of confusion, Miranda added, "Sorry, PSL is Port Shangri-La, where the Seagulls play, Palombo is the city where the Sehlats play, and—"

Holding up a hand, Beverly said, "I get it. So it was love at first sight?"

"Intrigue at first sight, certainly," Miranda said after considering it for a second. "He's one of those tiresome academics who aren't comfortable unless they've studied a subject all the way through, and so he had an amazing amount of baseball trivia in his head but no idea what any of it meant." She grinned. "It was rather charming. I started tutoring him, and then we agreed to get together for coffee the next day."

"How long did it take you to figure it out?"

"That we were in love?"

Beverly nodded.

"It took me a week—took him a skosh longer, I'm afraid. Again, he needed to study it thoroughly."

"I envy you—it took both Jack and me forever."

"And you and the captain fifteen years."

Thinking back to the days following Jack's death, Beverly thought, *There's an argument to be made that it's more like twenty.* Aloud, she just said, "Shall we continue the workout?"

Wincing, Miranda said, "Oh, bollocks, I'm sorry, love, I just got caught up in the gossiping."

"That's all right," Beverly said as she started doing a split.

Maybe I am glowing, she thought as she watched Miranda try to lower herself and having less success. *And why shouldn't I be?*

2

U.S.S. Titan
Gum Nebula

One day before the end of the universe

CAPTAIN WILLIAM RIKER STARED OUT THE WIN-
dow of his quarters, watching the unfamiliar stars
go by and reveling in their mystery.

He smiled, leaning back and stretching, the muscles and bones in his shoulders creaking and crack-
ing. It had been a long day, filled with the usual
hustle and bustle of running a starship, and preparation for the star system they'd be entering the following morning. The *Titan,* having completed its
maiden voyage to Romulus, was now on a mission

of exploration to the massive Gum Nebula in the Beta Quadrant, and the day had been spent in mission briefings, inspections of long-range sensors, and other preparatory duties. Four years after the Dominion War's end, it finally felt like Starfleet was getting back to basics: seeking out new life and going where no one had gone before.

Of course, "no one" was a relative term. They'd already found dozens of new life-forms out here and even reencountered some familiar ones. It was the assignment Riker felt he was born for.

Until he reported to the *Enterprise* at Farpoint Station, Will had been on the fast track to the captaincy, and no one expected him to be the first officer for more than a year or two. Yet three refused commands and fifteen years later, he was still there, still on the *Enterprise*—although now it was the E— still by the side of Jean-Luc Picard.

Thinking about it, he had been *too* gung-ho in many ways. He had the drive, he had the ambition, but Riker realized what he needed was the temperament. The officer he was fifteen years ago would've made an adequate captain. But the person who'd lived through all the missions was much better suited to be a ship commander.

He turned around and looked at the sleeping form of his new bride. Will Riker and Deanna Troi had been lovers on Betazed two decades ago. Reunited on the *Enterprise*-D, they served together as friends; it was only recently they realized they were meant to be together. They'd gotten married in two separate ceremonies: one on Earth, and a bittersweet one on Betazed, after Data's death.

They'd gotten subspace mail the previous day, including letters from Geordi and Beverly. The *Enterprise* was exploring as well, surveying the Gorsach system. *Good for them,* Riker had thought. After their experiences with the Borg, a simpler mission would be good for morale.

The one regret Riker had was that he wasn't there during the Borg encounter. Several times, the *Enterprise* had come across those cybernetic monsters, and Riker had always been there. Repressing a shudder, he remembered giving Worf the order to fire on the Borg cube, an action that—had it been successful—would have meant Picard's death. And, as always when he remembered that day, he cursed Q for so thoughtlessly tossing the *Enterprise* into the Borg's path in the first place, thus forcing him into the position of having to give an order that could have killed his captain. The death and destruction that could be laid at Q's feet for snapping his fingers and bringing the Federation to the Borg's undivided attention, taken in a fit of pique . . .

Riker sighed. It wasn't worth getting worked up over Q, any more than it was being frustrated over an ion storm or a sun going nova. Q simply was what he was—Riker probably knew that as well as anyone, having briefly been given the power of the Q. The best they could do was weather the storm until Q decided to leave.

"You're up."

Looking back over at the bed, he saw Deanna's sleepy eyes staring at him, her dark hair splayed on the pillow. Although she had spoken the words aloud, he had heard them in his mind a few seconds sooner, through the rapport they had shared since their days on Betazed. "Couldn't sleep," he said with a shrug. "Besides, we're supposed to be dropping out of warp pretty soon."

She got up and stood behind him, putting her arms under his, hands resting on his chest, staring at the stars through the port over his shoulder, on which her chin rested. "You regret not being on the *Enterprise* when they faced the Borg." It wasn't a question.

"To an extent. I suppose that's bound to keep happening every time we get a letter from someone or read a Starfleet dispatch."

"I'm sure Captain Picard feels the same way when he reads our letters or sees our reports as we file them."

Riker smiled. "Probably. I'm sure he'll get over it."

Before the conversation could be pursued, the stars stopped streaking by and normalized to twilights in the distant night sky, indicating—along with the subtle shift in the vibration of the deck plates that twenty-three years of Starfleet service had conditioned Riker to be able to read—that they had come out of warp and arrived at the Vela 3AG system.

As Riker recalled from the premission briefing, *Titan* was supposed to come into the system at an angle that would provide the captain with a view of the star, its fourth planet, and its ten moons from his cabin—which was the main reason why he'd awakened so early, so he could catch the vista he was promised.

Riker was surprised to see neither sun nor planet nor moons. Instead, a good portion of the lower-right-hand corner of his cabin port revealed a roiling mass of energy.

Gently disentangling himself from his wife, he touched a control on the nightstand. "Riker to bridge. Are you seeing what I'm seeing?"

Titan's second officer, Commander Tuvok, answered. *"If you are referring to the anomaly at bearing 197 mark 4, then the answer to your question would be yes."*

Smiling grimly at the Vulcan's reply, Riker said, "Yes, indeed, Mister Tuvok. What happened to Vela 3AG?"

"Only the outermost planetoids are still being picked up by our sensors—however, both have suffered temperature losses that bring them close to absolute zero, as well as tectonic stresses, neither of which matches what our long-range sensors picked up only yesterday."

"Can you tell me anything about the anomaly?"

"Sensors are not reading the anomaly's presence, Captain. While it has a visual component, it is not detectable by sensors at this range."

Riker moved over to the closet to grab a uniform, removing his bedclothes as he did so. "Send a class-one probe. I'm on my way up."

"Aye, sir."

"I don't like the sound of this," he said as he started getting dressed. "*Titan* has top-of-the-line sensors, and if *we* can't pick this up . . ."

Deanna walked up to him and put her hands on his shoulders. "We'll figure it out." And then she gave him a passionate kiss.

Riker enjoyed the kiss for several seconds before coming up for air and finishing putting on his uniform.

"Do you need me?" Deanna asked.

Grinning, Riker said, "Always."

She grinned right back. "I meant on the bridge."

"I wouldn't object, but no need to rush if you've got other priorities. If I *do* need you, I'll let you know."

She nodded. "Good luck, Will."

"Like you said, we'll figure this out." He smiled. "We've come across our share of bizarre spatial anomalies. I'm sure Tuvok will have fifteen possible scenarios by the time I reach the bridge."

Feeling a dread that belied his upbeat words—which he knew Deanna knew—Riker turned and headed for the bridge.

FIRST INTERLUDE

———◆———

The Continuum

Fifteen years before the end of the universe

"WOULD YOU MIND EXPLAINING YOURSELF, Q?"

He made a *tch* noise. "Actually, I would mind, as I'm far too complex a being to sum up in a brief explanation, and I'm not sure we have the kind of time for a long one. The ones will be needed *soon,* and—"

"Enough!" Q screamed. "You led us to believe that this was a serious matter, but then when we asked you to follow some simple instructions—"

"Simple instructions?" He stared at the assembled Q with his mouth agape. "You told me to give Riker the power of the Q."

"Actually," another Q said, "we told you to give Picard the power of the Q." He shrugged. "Not that it matters—one human's the same as another, really. Have you noticed they all look alike?"

"The *point* is," the first Q snapped, "you couldn't resist making a game of it, could you?"

He shrugged. "And why shouldn't I? Simply making Riker into a Q just like that was so . . ."

With a smile on her face, another Q—his favorite, the one he'd dallied with more than once—said, "Dull?" She'd always understood him best.

"Exactly!" he cried, thrilled at an advocate, especially thrilled that it was her. "Why not make the game interesting?"

"Two reasons," the first Q said angrily. "One, it is *not* a game. Two, I fail to see how mixing the histories of two worlds in a fantasy war can in any way be defined as 'interesting.'"

Q shook her head. "He has a point, Q."

He sighed. "Look, none of this matters. The point is, there's a very good chance that humans are the ones. If they are—"

"They aren't," the first Q said dismissively.

"Why are you so certain?" he asked.

"Why are *you*?" another Q retorted.

He said emphatically, "Because I've been *paying attention.* I've flitted about the cosmos spreading chaos in my wake, it's true, but what I've been doing is *observing.*"

"You truly expect us to believe that scientific curiosity prompts your meddling?"

"Of course not," he said, sounding offended. "Fun prompts my meddling. The scientific observation is merely a fortunate side effect. And from those observations," he added quickly before Q, Q, Q, Q, or Q could get a word in, "I have deduced that humanity stands the best chance of being the ones. All the signs point to it."

"Those signs are vague and indistinct," Q said, "and it's my considered opinion, Q, that you're using this surety as a feeble excuse to meddle further in human affairs."

He smiled. "Believe me, Q, I don't need an excuse, feeble or otherwise. If I just wanted to toy with this collection of ape-descended mammals, I would. But there's more *to* them, I'm sure of it!"

"Why this urgency?" his favorite Q asked.

"The Borg. You know as well as I that they are most likely to come across Them first, and if they do—"

"They won't," another Q—his least favorite—said.

"You're sure?"

"Of course I'm sure! I'm omnipotent."

He laughed. "So'm I, Q, and I'm telling you, I'm not so sure."

"Enough!" The first Q bellowed loudly enough to cause asteroids to explode. "You have tried the Q's patience enough, Q. You are banned from the Continuum while we deliberate on your fate."

That took him aback. "Banned?"

"Yes."

"But—but—you *can't*! The Continuum is my *home*! I can't—"

Q gave him the stare she always used when he annoyed her—which was fairly often, if it came to that—and said, "You're the one who enjoys flitting about the cosmos spreading chaos in your wake, dear. So go do it."

And then he was gone from the Continuum. Aghast, he tried to access it, but the way was blocked to him. As an experiment, he changed into a star-singer, which worked just fine. Then he turned into an Aldebaran serpent, a Belzoidian flea, a Traveler, and a baseball bat.

I still have my powers. I've simply been denied the ability to go home.

For good measure, he tried to get into the Continuum a second time. Then a third. No luck. He even tried concentrating, something he hadn't done in eons, and that didn't work, either.

He considered his next move. The Continuum could take ages to deliberate, and he wasn't sure the universe had that long. Even if it did, he was hardly about to wait around.

I may as well drop in on Jean-Luc. Make him an offer he can't refuse. After all, what better way to observe him and his merry band of outcasts and make sure they are the ones than by becoming one of their idiot crew?

3

Enterprise
En route to Gorsach IX

Two days before the end of the universe

CAPTAIN JEAN-LUC PICARD SAT IN HIS READY
room, perusing the daily report from his first officer. As alpha shift was winding down, he wanted
to make sure all was well. The department heads
had reported to Worf, and he had reported to the
captain.

The report was of less interest to Picard—it was
fairly standard, all one would expect given that the
Enterprise was on the ninth day of its journey to the
Gorsach star system—than the style in which it was
written. For the past decade and a half, Picard had

been reading reports by Will Riker, which were as comprehensive but also written in a manner that Picard could best describe as affable or easygoing. The captain, at first, had been put off by the tone, but he had grown accustomed to it. His previous first officer—Gilaad Ben Zoma on the *Stargazer*—had always been by the book in his reports, using dry, simple sentences. Riker's reports were more conversational, as if the commander was relating a story. Worf's reports were Klingon—taciturn, brusque—a refreshing change of pace.

The computer suddenly spoke. "The time is seventeen twenty-five hours."

Setting down the padd, Picard got to his feet and tugged his uniform jacket downward. "Thank you, computer." It was time for the mission briefing.

He exited the ready room to the sea of so many new faces. At conn, Lieutenant Joanna Faur had replaced Sara Nave, who was killed during the Borg mission. Commander Miranda Kadohata sat at ops instead of the familiar pale face of Data. The counselor's seat remained empty, but even if its occupant was present, it would be T'Lana, not Deanna Troi. Behind the also-empty first officer's chair, Zelik Leybenzon stood ramrod straight at the tactical station, the latest in a series of tactical officers the *Enterprise*-E had gone through since it launched eight years ago.

The most familiar face on the bridge was Worf. Jean-Luc Picard was not a man given to whimsy. Yet he wondered what the other *Enterprise* captains would have thought seeing a Klingon at their conn. For a moment the captain wondered if he was going soft.

Worf rose. "Counselor T'Lana, Doctor Crusher, and Commander La Forge have been paged, sir."

"Lieutenant Faur, you have the bridge."

The dark-haired woman said, "Aye, sir."

Entering the observation lounge, Picard swiftly crossed the room, barely noticing the stars as they streaked by at high warp. As he took his seat at the head of the table, he looked over to the models of all of the ships that bore the name *Enterprise* hanging on the bulkhead and wondered when he had stopped noticing. When had he stopped noticing how the stars looked? When had he stopped looking over his shoulder to make sure that his officers were following in his wake? And just what had Beverly put in his coffee this morning that he had suddenly gone nostalgic?

There was the culprit now.

"Captain." Beverly favored him with her "professional CMO smile" as she took her seat to his left.

"Doctor."

Worf took his seat to the captain's right, with Leybenzon beside him. Both men looked like coils ready to spring. He expected that from the first officer, who, despite four years in the Diplomatic Corps, would always be a Klingon warrior.

By contrast, Miranda Kadohata seemed relaxed as she took her seat next to Beverly. The commander had performed her admittedly routine duties over the past nine days admirably. But then, Data would not have chosen her if she wasn't up to his high standards for executive officer.

The doors parted, and Geordi La Forge and T'Lana entered. Simply put, Picard didn't entirely know what to make of his new counselor. The short, striking Vulcan woman had spent the entire Borg mission taking a position contrary to his. True, T'Lana's recommendations were logical and well thought out. It was also true that Picard's willing transformation into Locutus could charitably be called borderline insane; he had regained his humanity only because of Beverly's heroic action.

What concerns you, a voice nagged at the back of his head, *is that she doesn't completely trust you. That she* dared *to question your orders.* That could be beneficial, in truth. After all, his crew trusted him so completely that when they faced the Borg in Earth's past, it took an outsider—Lily Sloane—to see that he was turning into an Ahab-like obsessed madman. *Sometimes, the outsider's perspective can be useful.*

The captain considered his senior staff. T'Lana, seated next to Leybenzon, looked even smaller than her stature next to the security chief. Miranda seemed to hardly notice that La Forge had settled in beside her.

Folding his hands on the conference room table, Picard spoke: "As you know, we will be arriving tomorrow morning at Gorsach IX." Turning to his second officer, Picard said, "Commander Kadohata, what can you tell us about this world?"

A holographic display was activated in the table. Kadohata said, "The Gorsach system was first charted about two hundred years ago by a Tellarite astronomer, Efrak chim Gorsach." The display showed a sensor triagram of a star system with a yellow G-type star, and the orbital path for its ten planets, seventeen moons, six planetoids, and three asteroid belts. "The system was the test bed for a long-range probe he'd developed. Unfortunately, it broke down before he could successfully return the probe to Tellar. He lost his funding to build the probe series, which is why there aren't more systems named after him and why the information is spotty.

"According to various long-range probes that the Federation has sent that way over the intervening years—and our own long-range scans—the ninth planet is Class-M. There are also two gas giants in the system, the fourth and fifth planets. Those three are the only ones of the system's eleven planets that have *any* kind of atmosphere. The remaining eight are little more than barren rocks." Kadohata had been talking to the room, but now her gaze fell specifically on Picard. "Captain, I'd like to send class-twos to both gas giants. Gorsach IV's fairly standard, but the other one, the fifth planet, is quite large. It's possible it might be on the verge of igniting into a red dwarf."

Before Picard could answer the request, Leybenzon leaned forward in his chair. "Would that pose a danger to the ship?"

Giving the security chief a withering look,

Kadohata said, "The process takes centuries, Lieutenant. We should be fine."

"By all means, Commander," Picard said quickly, "send the probes."

Kadohata smiled. "Thank you, Captain." Then she grew serious again and touched a control in front of her. The hologram narrowed to the ninth planet. "Something else the probes have detected are considerable deposits of dilithium and topaline—worth looking into."

Worf added, "No signs of sentient life have been detected on the planet. Based on long-range sensor analysis, we have found a large canyon that is near some of the heaviest topaline and dilithium deposits."

"Are there any other signs of life?" Crusher asked.

"Lower animal life only," Worf said. "Impossible to say for certain beyond that."

"We'll be able to get a better notion of that once we're in-system, but I agree with Commander Worf that canyon's the best place to start a ground survey." Miranda deactivated the display.

"Very well," Picard said with a nod. "Number One, you will lead the away team."

"Thank you, Captain. With your permission, I will begin with a minimal team consisting of myself, Commander Kadohata, and Lieutenant Leybenzon. Once we have completed our initial survey, and determined that the location is secure, we will beam down a more complete scientific survey team and set up a base camp."

Kadohata said, "If you don't mind, Commander, I've some ideas about who should go on that team."

"The exact composition of the second team will be left to the discretion of the department heads," Worf said.

"Thank you, sir," Kadohata said with a pleased-looking nod.

Worf looked at the chief engineer. "Commander La Forge and I have discussed the physical aspects of the base camp."

La Forge nodded. "My guys are already on it. We should have a fully operational setup by the time you three finish the initial survey."

"If I may, Commander?" Leybenzon said. When Worf nodded, the security chief continued. "For the second team, I want one security guard for every scientist who beams down, and four to remain on rotating shifts at the base camp."

"Agreed," Worf said.

The captain said nothing—he always felt that the composition of an away team should be left to the person leading it—but he did notice that both La Forge and Crusher seemed a little surprised by the lieutenant's aggressive stance, not to mention Worf's support of it. Riker, Picard knew, would have likely taken a less cautious approach, but Worf had his own command style—honed over seven years as the *Enterprise*-D's security chief, and four years as Deep Space 9's strategic operations officer, which also included command of the *U.S.S. Defiant.*

However, Beverly could not let this pass without comment. "Don't you both think that's a little extreme? We're exploring a new world, not securing a beachhead."

"We are venturing into the unknown, Doctor," Worf said. "It is prudent to take every precaution. Experience has shown us that the missions that seem on the surface to be routine are the ones that pose the most danger."

"Murphy's Law and all that," Kadohata said. "'Whatever can go wrong, will go wrong.'"

Looking back at Crusher, Worf said, "I believe that Lieutenant Leybenzon's request is reasonable under the circumstances."

Picard suppressed a smile as he leaned back in his chair. He enjoyed watching the new dynamic between his senior staff.

Over the course of fifteen years, the *Enterprise*'s senior staff had become a well-oiled machine. Everyone knew what to expect from everyone else. On his first command, the *Stargazer,* turnover was the rule. As a young captain he relished the challenge of managing his staff, of making sure everyone was heard.

The captain noted that T'Lana had been silent during the briefing, and he wanted to hear her input. "Counselor, is there anything you wish to add?"

T'Lana raised an eyebrow, as if surprised at the question. "I do not believe so, Captain."

He tried a different tack. "How is the crew's spirit?"

Picard had feared some sort of rejoinder questioning the wisdom of using the word "spirit" in this context, but T'Lana simply lowered her eyebrow and said, "I would say encouraged, Captain. This is a mission with which they all feel comfortable. My impression is one of satisfaction, that the crew feels that they are fulfilling the duties that they joined Starfleet to perform."

"Thank you, Counselor." Picard stood, tugging down on his uniform jacket. "If there is nothing else?"

Nobody said anything.

"Very well, then. We should make orbit at zero-seven hundred tomorrow, at which point, the away team will disembark from Transporter Room 3. Dismissed."

La Forge said, "Anyone up for some dinner?"

The captain considered accepting, then decided it was best if he caught up on his reports—he'd done enough to put himself on Admiral Janeway's bad side, and it wouldn't do to antagonize her further. "I'm afraid I must decline, Mister La Forge, but thank you."

"I'm game," Kadohata said.

"Uh, okay," La Forge said.

Miranda added, "I'm near starved, to be honest."

Crusher smiled. "Well, we can't let that happen."

"And I promise I won't bring along baby pictures," Kadohata added with a smile.

"In that case, I will join you," Worf deadpanned. Picard had to repress a smile of his own. Her first few days on board, Miranda had been eagerly showing images of her twins to anyone who'd stand still long enough—and even some who didn't. To Picard, Colin Farrenga and Sylvana Kadohata looked like most human babies: akin to stewed prunes. He of course said nothing of the sort to his new second officer, instead providing her with some encouraging cliché or other.

T'Lana moved toward the exit. "I must decline, as well, Commander, as I have several appointments throughout the evening. If you will excuse me." She exited quickly.

La Forge turned his artificial eyes toward Leybenzon. "Lieutenant? Up for a meal?"

"Your offer is generous, but I'm afraid that I have a security detail that needs to be in proper working order when we arrive at Gorsach IX." With that, he turned on his heel and departed.

La Forge mused, "He must be *great* fun at parties."

SECOND INTERLUDE

The Continuum

Thirteen years before the end of the universe

Q HAD TO ADMIT TO BEING SURPRISED AT THESE humans whom Q had decided to throw in his lot with.

In all honesty, Q was worried about Q. The old boy, he had thought recently, was finally losing it. All that goofing off over the millennia had finally turned his little Q brain into toast. When he started obsessing over humans, Q was convinced it was over. After all, what was the big deal? Humans had all those extra appendages, shockingly limited vision (in every sense of the word), and less brain capacity than the average virus.

Q hadn't learned his lesson, Q argued, and needed to be punished. Banishment alone wouldn't do it—the first thing he did after they banished him was introduce the humans to the *Borg*. That proved he had gone completely bonkers and needed to be taught a lesson.

The rest of the Continuum agreed. Q had asked for leniency, which Q thought was sweet of her, but she'd always had a soft spot for Q. Q, however, was insistent that he be made mortal, forced to live out his life as one of the many creatures he had loved to torment over the centuries. Perhaps then he would learn his lesson.

Of course, the first thing Q did was show he hadn't learned a damn thing: of all the mortals he could have requested to be made into, he chose the humans and asked to be sent to that ridiculous ship he was obsessed with.

Q, naturally, kept an eye on him. It was possible that he would *eventually* learn his lesson.

Instead, Q found himself learning something, which rather took him aback.

The final straw came when Q actually committed a selfless act. The Calamarain had learned of Q's fallen state and—not surprising, given what Q did to them several moments ago—tried to kill him. The humans, despite the fact that Q had made their lives miserable for the past few moments, actually protected him.

Q, rather than let them risk their lives, decided to sacrifice himself.

Did he really learn his lesson? Q wondered as

the Calamarain moved in and the humans tried to use their primitive matter-transferral technology to rescue Q. *Or is he simply preserving the humans in his silly quest to be sure that they're the ones?*

It didn't matter, though, what the reasons were. Q felt strongly enough about these humans that he was about to sacrifice himself to save them. A Q would die. Not as traumatic an occurrence if he had not already been punished, but still an event.

Q decided to stop it. Something more was at work here. *And maybe there's more to what Q's saying than we all realized. Maybe it's time we took his notion seriously.*

As he took on human form in order to better communicate with Q—he gave himself blond hair, blue eyes, and a height commensurate with the human form that Q generally took on—he moved himself into the little ship Q had stolen and decided to have a heart-to-heart talk, one omnipotent being to another. . . .

4

———

Bravo Station
Sector 221, Alpha Quadrant

One day before the end of the universe

ADMIRAL ELIZABETH PAULA SHELBY SCROLLED through the latest set of dispatches from Starfleet. The *U.S.S. Sugihara* had a complete report on a neutron star that it observed in Sector 109-G. Starbase 152 reported a force-six ion storm blowing through. Outpost 22 along the Romulan Neutral Zone had the latest report on a ship apparently full of Reman refugees that was proceeding at minimum warp toward it, and any number of other reports. Some of the dispatches Shelby recognized, having created them herself: reports on Sector 221-G, the area of space that Shelby and Bravo were responsible for.

However, two sets of dispatches got her attention: the ones from the *Enterprise* and the *Titan.*

The latter was one that Shelby enjoyed reading. *Titan* was under the command of Will Riker. Shelby had first met Riker on the *Enterprise*-D, when she was Starfleet's point person in their efforts to stop the Borg. She had thought herself the logical replacement for Riker as first officer when he took command of the *Melbourne.* Riker had not accepted the post, for which Shelby had castigated him more than once. After the Borg were stopped, Shelby went on to become first officer of the *Chekov,* and later the *Excalibur,* and she served as captain of the *Exeter* and the *Trident.* Now Shelby was an admiral in charge of an entire sector and a space station. She'd even gotten married, to a fellow Starfleet officer, one of the captains under her command, in fact.

Looking back, Shelby was embarrassed at the way she'd behaved toward Riker. True, the two of them didn't exactly see eye to eye—she, a brash lieutenant commander so full of herself that she could not understand why *everyone* just didn't do it her way. Marriage to another being equally headstrong sometimes left her wondering if a little more looking before leaping might be a good idea. She'd consider it for all of two or three seconds and then leap into the fray, regs be damned. Strange, she would have never thought Picard would do the same thing. But here it was in front of her. Jean-Luc Picard had disobeyed a direct order. The *Enterprise* had faced the Borg. But these were not the creatures she had studied. These Borg were closer to the monsters that had lived under her bed as a child. These Borg killed on sight. The thought filled Admiral Shelby with a dread she could not name.

"Ops to Admiral Shelby."

She tapped her combadge. "Go ahead."

"Admiral, this is Ensign Galeckas. Something's happened to the Inwood."

Shelby blinked. The *Inwood* was the runabout that had just departed Bravo with crew replacements for Shelby's former command, the *Trident*. "Define 'something.'"

"I can't, Admiral. According to what we can see out the ports, there's some kind of weird rift in space between us and the Inwood's *heading."*

"Ensign, Bravo Station has state-of-the-art sensors that can detect the individual grains of sand on a planet six light-years away. Would you mind explaining why you had to look out a port?"

"I'm sorry, Admiral, but—well, those state-of-the-art sensors aren't picking up a damn thing. The only reason we know the rift is there is because we can see it."

"How can something be in the visible spectrum and not be detected by sensors?"

"We've, uh, been asking ourselves that, sir."

Sighing, Shelby got up from her desk. "I'll be right up."

If nothing else, Shelby figured this was preferable to driving herself crazy wondering how and why the Borg changed. . . .

5

———◆———

Enterprise
En route to Gorsach IX

Two days before the end of the universe

LA FORGE HAD GONE DOWN TO THE CREW LOUNGE
with Worf, Crusher, and Kadohata straight from the
mission briefing. The chief engineer had spent the
first half of the day talking with Worf about what
would be required for the base camp on Gorsach IX,
and the second half of the day processing those requirements with Taurik, his deputy chief engineer.
He had skipped lunch in between those two lengthy
conversations and so could use a good meal.

Being turned down by T'Lana and Leybenzon
had been a disappointment. La Forge had spent

most of the time since they'd set out for Gorsach tweaking the fixes made in drydock after their encounter with the Borg and also breaking in some new engineers. Tonight was really Geordi's first chance to relax and have an in-depth chat with the newest members of the *Enterprise* senior staff before the Gorsach mission kicked into high gear.

"All right, I recall that Ten-Forward on the D was called that because it was on deck ten in the forward section. Why is this called the Riding Club?" asked Kadohata.

"The full name," Crusher said, "is the Happy Bottom Riding Club. Will was the one who came up with the name."

Worf got a sour look on his face. La Forge recalled that Worf had refused to use "that name."

Crusher explained, "The original was run by a woman named Pancho Barnes in California on Earth about four or five hundred years ago. It was near a base for test pilots of ancient fixed-wing aircraft, in a remote desert area with a ranch, rodeo field, dance hall, and a restaurant. Barnes offered a free steak dinner to anyone who flew faster than the speed of sound. A Captain Chuck Yeager?"— Beverly looked to Geordi for confirmation; the engineer nodded, while his Klingon friend continued to glower—"was the first, dozens more followed. Legend has it that many of the original astronauts were recruited at Barnes's bar."

Smiling, Kadohata asked, "When did you become such an expert?"

"I'm not," Crusher said emphatically, "but I heard Will talk about it *endlessly*, particularly when he was trying to sell the captain the name. For a while, we were still calling it Ten-Forward, I suppose out of habit. Will kept arguing, 'New ship, new name.'"

Worf grunted and mumbled something.

Miranda said, "I didn't get that."

"For some reason, Worf thinks it was all an elaborate practical joke, a parting shot by Captain Riker," Crusher explained. She leaned in closer to Miranda and whispered, "Just pay no attention to Worf."

The Riding Club's host, Jordan, came by. A tall, attractive man with a sharp widow's peak, he'd been the steward in the lounge for the last several years. Guinan, who had managed Ten-Forward on the D, had moved on to other things. La Forge was surprised to see her at Riker and Troi's wedding a few months ago. It was as if she had never left, and all things considered, Geordi wouldn't be surprised to see Guinan one day behind the bar like she had never left.

Since the crew lounge had been christened "The Happy Bottom Riding Club," Jordan had embraced Barnes's tradition of attaching items and two-dimensional images to the wall behind the bar. The first so honored was Guinan, with a two-D photo of her in one of her infamous hats—the yellow one. Then he'd added an actual horseshoe, a portrait of Barnes, an early-twentieth-century map of southern California indicating the original Riding Club's location, framed pictures of crew members who had been killed in action since the double E was launched, a mission patch from Archer's *Enterprise,* a copy of the original club's liquor license, and a replica of the dedication plaque of Kirk's *Enterprise.* The captain had even gotten into the act, donating his *d'k tahg.* Each time something was added, Jordan would regale whoever was sitting at the bar with a tale about it, and pity any newbie who dared to ask, "What's with the wall?"

"Let me guess," Jordan said as he approached the table. He looked at the group. "For our XO, steamed *hasperat* and iced tea. The doctor will have *lIngta'* lo mein with a *grakizh* salad and quinine water. Geordi will have jambalaya *à la* Sisko with *raktajino.* And Commander, I have fresh *taknar* gizzards with *grapok* sauce and your usual prune juice."

La Forge looked at his dinner mates. "He's good."

Kadohata said, "Jordan, if I have to eat one more steamed dish I'm going to break down and cry." She turned to La Forge. "Geordi, do you mind if I copy you and try the jambalaya?"

Wincing at the familiarity of using his first name, La Forge shrugged. "No."

"Cheers, then, I'll have that."

"Still the iced tea?" Jordan asked.

"Yes, thank you."

Jordan went to place the order. Crusher gave the others a conspiratorial look. "I think we're getting predictable in our old age. Worf, Jordan even knew what you wanted."

"When I dine in the company of others," Worf said, "I tend toward *taknar* gizzards as they are the Klingon food that tends to provoke the least . . . extreme response in others."

La Forge could have sworn he saw a smile play on the Klingon's lips. *He's definitely mellowed.*

So why the hell haven't I? He had never been one for formality, having always been content to let even his engineers call him by his first name. He didn't understand why Miranda calling him "Geordi" made him skittish.

"By the way, Geordi," Kadohata said, and damned if La Forge didn't wince *again,* "good job on the repair work. I read the damage reports when I was en route to Starbase 815 from Cestus, and I would've imagined the repairs would take weeks, plural, but your lot got the Corps to move . . . well, it was amazing."

"Thanks," La Forge said.

Kadohata said with a roll of her eyes, "Our chief engineer never met a repair estimate."

"You will find, Commander," Worf said, "that *all* standards are high on the *Enterprise.*"

"Is that why you came back?" Kadohata asked. "Forgive my asking, but I had thought you were pursuing a career in diplomacy."

Before Worf could answer, Jordan returned with everyone's drinks. La Forge quickly grabbed his *raktajino* mug and took a sip of the powerful Kling-on coffee. While La Forge didn't think much of Klingon food—too much squirming and moving—

the Klingons knew how to make a cup of coffee.

After their drinks were served, Worf explained, "Becoming an ambassador was never meant to be a permanent career. The position was offered by Chancellor Martok and Admiral Ross, and I therefore could not refuse. I was able to serve both the Federation and the Empire—but when the opportunity presented itself, I returned to Starfleet."

"Well, I, for one, am grateful," La Forge said, holding up his mug as if proposing a toast. "Can you imagine what Command would've sent over as a first officer if you weren't available after Data . . . ?" The words caught in La Forge's throat.

Crusher leaned forward. "Geordi?"

"Hm? Yeah, I'm fine. It's just—" He let out a long breath. "It's been tough getting used to it, y'know? Data was supposed to outlive all of us." La Forge rushed on. "It's all right, though. Honestly, with B-4 trundled off to the Daystrom Institute, it's gotten easier. I think the toughest part of losing Data was having his evil twin around."

Crusher smiled. "I thought Lore was his evil twin."

"Yeah, good point," La Forge said, grateful for the opportunity to laugh. "I guess B-4's the idiot cousin?"

"Every family has one," Miranda said. "Vicenzo has this loony named Fred for a cousin, and—"

Before Kadohata could go on about her cousin-in-law, Jordan came by with the food. La Forge saw that while *taknar* gizzards were more palatable than most Klingon food, they were still pretty disgusting. Luckily, the spices in the two jambalayas overpowered the smell of the gizzards that just sat there oddly glazing on Worf's plate. Geordi wondered when Worf stopped eating non-Klingon dishes. What happened to Worf while he was on DS9? Always taciturn and extremely private, La Forge never asked. So much change . . .

Well, except for the prune juice. Guinan had introduced Worf to the beverage, which the Klingon had proudly pronounced to be "a warrior's drink." It had become a running joke on the *Enterprise*-D, but Worf had the last laugh, as prune juice had become a major export to the Klingon Empire in recent years.

Looking at Crusher's dish, Worf said, "That is a most—unique method of preparing *lIngta'*, Doctor."

"It can be fun to mix and match," Beverly said as she speared her lo mein with a fork. "If I remember correctly, the jambalaya that Geordi and Miranda are eating uses spices from Andor, meat from a free-range animal on Zalda, and Bolian rice."

"Kriosian rice, actually," Worf said. La Forge shot him a surprised glance, and Worf added, "Captain Sisko prepared the meal on several occasions on DS9. He said the Kriosian rice was . . . fluffier." He took a bite, chewed, swallowed, and frowned. "The replicators have never been able to re-create it precisely."

Kadohata had an expression of disbelief and joy on her face, as she had just taken her first bite.

"You mean there's a version of this that's even *better*? This is heavenly!"

Worf returned to the previous topic of conversation. "Sending B-4 to the Daystrom Institute was a prudent course of action. It was as if Data's *jatyIn* was aboard the vessel."

"Except it was just like Data's body but not his personality," La Forge said.

"Unacceptable," Worf said.

"It was a way of keeping Data alive. Preserving his memory—literally, since Data downloaded his memories into B-4."

La Forge pushed his food around.

Miranda dared to break the silence. "I don't understand, not his personality?"

Geordi shook his head. "We never figured out Graves's trick." Ira Graves, before his death, had downloaded his personality into Data's body. But Graves had left no documentation on the procedure, so it wasn't replicable. "This was just a straight data dump. B-4 had all of Data's knowledge . . . B-4 wouldn't get Data's personality from that, any more than Data would have Lore's or Lal's personality."

Kadohata gulped down most of her iced tea—the jambalaya was very spicy. "Why did Data do that?"

"He thought it would help B-4 evolve, become more like . . . it only confused B-4."

La Forge chuckled. "Remember when Data grew the beard?"

Crusher frowned. "No."

"It was when you were at Starfleet Medical,"

La Forge said. "And he only showed it to me and Deanna. It was right after Will grew his, and I guess he wanted to experiment."

"He didn't only show it to you and Counselor Troi," Miranda added.

Crusher shot her a glance. "You're kidding."

"He reported to the sensor room with it." Kadohata shook her head. "It was a nightmare. Here we were, three junior-grade lieutenants. One was newly assigned, along with me and—I don't remember her name." Her eyes widened. "Oh, this is awful, we served together for three years—Rothman! Anyway, Data walked in with the beard, and we were stunned. It was awful. He was our superior officer, after all; we could hardly tell him he looked like a ferret grew on his chin. We couldn't . . . it would've broken his heart."

"Commander Data," Worf said, "did not have a heart."

"Yeah," La Forge said, "but you still couldn't laugh at him. It'd be like kicking a puppy."

Again, Worf gave that small smile. "Speak for yourself."

It took La Forge a moment to realize that the Klingon was pulling his leg. "Yeah, well, I would've liked to have seen *you* laugh at him."

"I would never have done so to a superior officer," Worf said archly. Then the smile returned. "In his presence."

"That was our solution," Kadohata said. "As soon as we'd all given our reports, he left, and we collapsed. I think we laughed for a full two minutes. I couldn't breathe for the next hour."

"I still remember when Q made him laugh," La Forge said. "Well, okay, to be fair, he didn't *make* him laugh. He *let* him laugh. I think it's the one and only time Q did something nice."

"That assumes that Q's purpose was not to humiliate Data in much the same way laughing at his beard would have done," Worf added sourly.

"Well, then, it didn't work," La Forge said with a shrug.

Picking up his prune juice, Worf said, "Q failing in his stated goals would not be . . . inconsistent."

Crusher nodded. "For someone claiming to be omnipotent, he seemed to miss out on the basics."

"Well, Data appreciated it," La Forge said. "I can tell you that much. I'd say that's the happiest he was before the emotion chip."

They started telling Data stories. Kadohata shared a few from the perspective of someone who worked directly under the android. La Forge told some of his own: Data throwing a jazz funeral party for La Forge and another officer who were both believed killed; Data performing *Henry V* for the crew; Data and La Forge's Sherlock Holmes program getting out of control. And so many more.

Doctor Crusher told them about teaching Data to dance in preparation for being the "father of the bride" at the Ishikawa-O'Brien wedding. ("You dance?" Kadohata said, sounding stunned. Crusher sighed resignedly and said, "*Yes,* I dance.") Worf even had a Klingon tale, telling how Data helped him come to an important decision about the clone of Kahless.

By the time Jordan came to clear the plates, Worf had decided that Data should be remembered in song, "like the true warrior he was." Kadohata was pressing the Klingon on who should write the song. Doctor Crusher and Commander La Forge looked horrified when Worf suggested, "Perhaps a Klingon opera."

They were interrupted by raucous laughter as the doors opened. About a dozen people came in, all in the gold-trim uniforms of operations. La Forge recognized a few of them—Stolovitzky and Kapsis, both from security—but the one who stood out was Zelik Leybenzon. Thanks to his ocular implants, La Forge didn't "see" people by face but rather by body chemistry.

Leybenzon was laughing, louder than any of them. La Forge would have bet all the gold-pressed latinum in the universe that there was a higher likelihood of Worf showing up for duty in a pink tutu than their new tactical officer even knowing how to laugh.

"The amazing thing," Leybenzon said between guffaws, "was that he had no idea how hideous it was. He was so *proud* of what he'd done, and we could only just *stand* there." He slapped one of the guards La Forge didn't know on the back, causing the young ensign to stumble forward.

The group moved to the far corner of the Riding

Club and pushed several tables together. Leybenzon walked over to Jordan and put an arm around the steward's shoulder.

"Barkeep, I would like to request a round of drinks for my people. Stolichnaya, if you would be so kind, okay?"

"Syntheholic, yes?"

Leybenzon let out a long breath, then looked at the guards, who were taking their seats. "I suppose it will be necessary to settle for such, yes. I fear for these poor young fools and their ability to properly metabolize."

"I especially don't want them metabolizing all over the carpet."

That prompted a braying chortle from Leybenzon, who removed his arm from Jordan's shoulder and went to join his group.

La Forge asked, "Is that the same guy who's been at tactical?"

"He *is* a bit of a cold fish, isn't he?" Kadohata said.

"Not right now, he isn't." La Forge didn't bother trying to hide the bitterness in his voice. He had invited Leybenzon down here as a friendly gesture, and instead of just declining politely the way the captain and the counselor did, he out-and-out lied. That didn't sit well with Geordi La Forge at *all*.

Worf said, "In my conversations with Lieutenant Leybenzon, he has indicated that his preferred style of command is to drive his personnel hard while on duty—and reward them while off."

"Hang on," Kadohata said, "you've had *conversations* with him?"

"Several."

La Forge said, "But as part of your duty as first officer, right?"

"Not entirely. We have shared drinks here on several occasions." Again the smile. "He has the stomach for bloodwine—rare in a human."

"Huh." La Forge shook his head. "Somehow, it just figures that *you* would get along with him." He said it with a smile to make it clear that he was kidding.

Crusher put in, "I haven't been able to get him to take his physical. I mentioned it to him this morning, all but made it a direct order. He still didn't show up in sickbay."

Worf straightened. "I *will* make it a direct order, Doctor, rest assured."

La Forge was glad to see that. He'd hate for Worf to give the jerk special treatment just because they'd shared a couple of bloodwines. *But then, Worf wouldn't do that.*

"It's amazing," Crusher said, looking over at the corner Leybenzon and his people had taken over. "It's like he's a completely different person."

"Maybe he is," La Forge muttered.

"Bridge to Kadohata."

The second officer looked up at the voice of Ensign Vogel, the beta-shift tactical officer, and tapped her combadge. "Go ahead."

"Commander, you have a personal message from Cestus III."

"What's the time?"

"It's nineteen hundred hours, sir."

"Blast and damn, I lost track of time. It's Vicenzo. I'll take it in my quarters, Ensign."

"Aye, sir," Vogel said.

Miranda dabbed her mouth with her napkin. "If you'll excuse me. Geordi, thank you, this was a lovely idea."

Crusher got up. "I think I'm going to get going. I still haven't processed all the physicals." She grinned. "I wouldn't want to get *my* replacement as head of Starfleet Medical angry."

"G'night, Beverly."

"I will depart as well," Worf said.

Looking over at the security personnel, La Forge said, "I think I'll stick around. Maybe Leybenzon *is* a different person, and maybe this one's friendlier."

Worf inclined his head. "As you wish. Good night, Commander."

La Forge shook his head as the Klingon departed the lounge. *He's second in command, and he still calls me by rank, and Kadohata uses my first name.*

Of course, he was still thinking of her by her last name, even though she'd said to call her Miranda.

La Forge walked over to the far corner of the Riding Club. Leybenzon was holding court, sitting with his back to the wall, looking out over the entire lounge. His body temperature had gone up, no doubt a by-product of the syntheholic vodka he was drinking,

"—the Jem'Hadar just stood there, with his tube

leaking white all over the cave floor. He tried to put it back, and it squirted right in his eye!"

Several of the officers laughed at that.

"The poor fool was blinded, so I had the time to unholster my phaser—barely. The Jem'Hadar was killed a moment later, but as he fell, the white squirted right onto my uniform." He shook his head. "The replicator was down, and relief was not due for a week. And all we had to eat were combat rations, which are the product of the devil himself."

"Definitely," one guard commented.

"Hey, I *like* combat rations!"

"I'd sooner eat wheat paste!"

Leybenzon chuckled. "I *have* eaten wheat paste, my young friend, and I can assure you, combat rations are worse."

That was an entrée La Forge couldn't resist. "I gotta ask, Lieutenant—when did you have cause to eat wheat paste?"

Immediately, the chair shot out from under him and Leybenzon stood up straight. His voice, which had been a bit higher pitched during his entire time in the Riding Club, was now back in the deeper range that he used on duty. "May I help you, Commander?"

Holding up his hands, La Forge said, "At ease, Lieutenant. We're all off duty here. I couldn't help overhearing, and I was wondering when you ate wheat paste."

With his optical implants, La Forge was able to see Leybenzon's pulse quicken, though whether it was due to anger, confusion, or just the drink, La Forge couldn't be sure.

Then Stolovitzky, Leybenzon's deputy, said, "I wouldn't mind hearing that one myself."

After a moment, Leybenzon shook his head and chuckled. "Very well, it seems only fair. And I make it a practice to rarely refuse the request of a superior officer."

La Forge cocked an eyebrow. "Rarely?"

Holding up one finger, Leybenzon said, "One story at a time, Commander." He kicked the chair that Kapsis was sitting in and said, "Make room for our chief engineer."

Kapsis blinked several times, as if coming out of a daze. "Hm? Oh, yes, sir." He quickly got up.

Leaning over and whispering almost conpiratorially, Leybenzon said, "It is sad when the lower ranks cannot handle even false vodka. Speaking of which!" He leaned over at the table, grabbed the bottle of syntheholic vodka and a glass, and poured some. "You must drink if you are to hear the story."

La Forge accepted the drink, then sat. "Can't argue with that." He took a sip, and suddenly he felt like a warp core breach went off in his head. "Whoa."

Everyone laughed at La Forge's reaction, and he joined in with them a moment later, once the effect wore off. The chief engineer had not been much of a vodka aficionado, and the taste of this made him wonder what kind of punch the real thing packed. He was still recovering from the last time he'd seen

Montgomery Scott and the old engineer forced him to drink Scotch. . . .

His voice getting progressively higher, Leybenzon started his tale. "Now then—the wheat paste. It all began when the *Andromeda* was assigned to Minos Korva during the war. The Cardassians . . ."

Leaning back in his chair, La Forge listened to the story, which was followed by another. Then several of the security personnel told stories of their own, and La Forge even regaled them with a recent mission to a planet called Tezwa, which involved La Forge and a team of engineers and security personnel climbing a mountain.

What impressed him most, though, was Leybenzon. However much of a jackass he was on duty, off duty he was a raconteur, and, more to the point, he inspired loyalty in his people. La Forge had been supervising a large staff for a decade and a half now, and he knew when people responded to leadership. He would have never used Leybenzon's methods, but that didn't make them bad ones.

Geordi also realized that Leybenzon *hadn't* lied. He had said he needed to get the security staff into shape. This was part of how he was doing it.

6

I.K.S. Gorkon
Klingon Empire

One day before the end of the universe

CAPTAIN KLAG, SON OF M'RAQ, PROWLED THE inner decks of the *I.K.S. Gorkon,* unwilling to sleep.

He was walking through the soldiers' barracks, located on the mighty vessel's centralmost deck amid a labyrinth of corridors, each wall consisting of groups of five stacked two-meter-by-one-meter bunks, each group representing a squad. Like all the *Chancellor*-class vessels, the *Gorkon* carried a complement of over twenty-seven hundred warriors, fifteen hundred of whom were troops, divided into twenty companies. Each company was led by a

QaS DevwI', or troop commander, with fifteen five-troop squads per company.

Striding through the corridor that contained the bunks for Fourth Company, Klag came upon the fifteen empty bunks that belonged to the fiftieth, fifty-first, and fifty-second squads.

For three days, the *I.K.S. Gorkon* had been searching for the Kinshaya pirates who had raided an outpost in the Mempa sector and taken several Klingons prisoner—including Klag's first officer and the soldiers from those three squads. If the warriors were dead—as Klag hoped to be the case, for no Klingon wanted to be taken prisoner—then they would be avenged. If the Kinshaya had not allowed them to die—which Klag considered likely—then they would have the first opportunity to avenge the insult once they were liberated.

Either way, he swore to the soldiers via their empty bunks, *the Kinshaya* petaQpu' *will pay for what they have done. This I swear.*

That the Kinshaya had engaged in such daring tactics bespoke how badly things were going for them. Long an irritant to the Klingon Empire—the equivalent of a *glob* fly buzzing at their faces—about a year after the Dominion War's end, the Kinshaya decided to raise their voices. First they conquered the Kreel—a minor bordering nation that, rather than actively fight the Klingons, picked away at their conquests like a *kretlach* hovering over a *lIngta'* corpse. Adding the Kreel's resources to their own had made the Kinshaya much more formidable—though still just an irritant.

And now they have taken my second-in-command and fifteen of my warriors.

Klag was no stranger to loss. Death was a warrior's constant companion, and if the commander was indeed dead, it wouldn't be the first time Klag screamed a warning to the Black Fleet that his first officer was about to join them.

But he preferred such a death to come at the hands of a *worthy* foe.

Continuing down the corridor, Klag came across the soldiers of the fifty-third, fifty-fourth, and fifty-fifth playing a game of *grinnak.* At the captain's approach, all fifteen of them dropped their tokens and slips and stood at attention.

"Stand easy," Klag said. Then he broke into a smile. "Who is winning?"

Leader Krytak of the fifty-fourth said, "It certainly isn't me, sir."

"I've warned you in the past, Leader, about playing too many tokens at once."

"Krytak's not so good at heeding warnings, Captain." Those words were spoken by the leader of the fifty-third, whose name Klag could not remember. Indeed, he remembered Krytak only because, during a campaign a year ago, Klag had seen Krytak playing *grinnak* with several officers. That had surprised Klag at the time—officers and soldiers didn't often mix like that—but one of the officers was a Housemate of Krytak's, and so the soldier joined the game. That officer had since been killed during the retaking of a moon by a group of criminals, and Krytak's invitation to that particular *grinnak* game was rescinded, leaving him to lose only to his fellow soldiers.

Putting a hand on Krytak's shoulder, Klag said sagely, "Such is the mark of a fine warrior—and a terrible *grinnak* player."

Most of the soldiers laughed at that. The leader of the fifty-third was the only one who didn't. "Sir, permission to ask a question."

The captain knew precisely what the question was. These three squads were on their sleep cycle, but they were obviously as unwilling to sleep—as their captain was—for the same reasons. Klag said, "We have not found the Kinshaya yet, Leader. I've already spoken with your *QaS DevwI'* and told her that the remainder of Fourth Company will be at the forefront of whatever action we take against them."

Krytak said, "Thank you, sir."

"Your loyalty does you credit."

"It's not just that, sir," said the leader of the fifty-fifth. "That should've been us, sir."

Klag growled. "Explain."

The leader of the fifty-fifth grew nervous at his captain's anger. "Last week, sir, in the mess hall, sir, we had a wager. See, there was that bad batch of bloodwine, sir, that had gone off, remember, sir?"

Klag had a vague recollection of the quartermaster mentioning something about a bad batch arriving on the ship, but Klag—who had his own private stock—hadn't paid much attention. "Continue."

"We had a wager, sir, to see who could drink the most before throwing up, sir." Suddenly sounding prideful, the leader said, "We won, sir."

Now Klag understood. "And the wager was to switch assignments."

Krytak jumped in. "We didn't think going to that base would be a particularly glorious task, Captain."

Quoting Kahless, Klag said, "'Glory comes from unexpected sources,' Leader. If it was expected, it isn't especially glorious."

"I'll remember that, sir."

Smiling, Klag said, "Along with remembering not to play too many tokens at once, I'm sure. Continue with your game, my warriors. You will have the opportunity to reclaim your honor soon enough!"

The soldiers all cheered in response to that and went back to their game.

Klag continued down the corridor, only to hear his communicator go off. *Bridge to captain.*

It was the voice of the second-shift commander, who was new. Klag couldn't remember her name, either. "Speak."

"Sir, we have detected a warp trail that matches that of the Kinshaya ship, and it leads to the Trakliv system. We have changed course to intercept and will arrive in one hour."

"Good. I will be on the bridge shortly."

Klag strode more quickly through the corridors of his ship. Four years later, he still took immense pride in captaining this vessel, a goal that he had thought unattainable for so long, after his seemingly endless service on the *Pagh* under the terminally incompetent Captain Kargan.

However, Kargan was kind enough to die in the Dominion War, clearing the way for Klag at last to achieve his own command, and one of the top new vessels in the Defense Force on top of that.

As he worked his way forward through the *Gorkon,* Klag thought back on one of the few happy memories he had of his tour on the *Pagh:* the unlikely friendship he'd developed with a human Starfleeter named William Riker. When Klag was still second officer on the *Pagh,* an officer exchange program with the Federation had sent Riker, then the first officer of the *Enterprise,* to take over as second-in-command. Though his tenure had been brief, it had made a lasting impression on Klag, whose prior opinion of humans was low, to say the least.

After his transfer back to the *Enterprise,* he had remained in touch with Riker.

Klag was promoted to first officer. Both he and Riker retained their positions for far too long—Riker by choice, Klag by Kargan's decision to keep his first by his side in order to cover his own pathetic inability to command.

As Klag entered the bridge of *his* ship, he thought proudly, *Commanding this ship is where I belong.*

Even as the door rumbled aside to let Klag in, the second-shift operations officer reported, "Sir, something is wrong!"

The words had been directed at the second-shift commander seated in front of him, so the young officer was rather shocked when Klag asked, "What is it, Ensign?"

Whirling around, the ensign composed himself quickly. "Sir, the warp trail of the Kinshaya vessel has come to an end very abruptly—and the Trakliv system is *gone!*"

The pilot said, "Confirmed. There's . . . something else where the system used to be."

"On screen," Klag said as he walked to the front of the bridge. As with most Klingon vessels, there was an open space between the command chair and the viewscreen, with all the other bridge officers behind him. The placement of the bridge at the very front of the ship reinforced the Klingon ideal that the captain led his warriors into battle. The bridge design proved the captain trusted his crew enough to turn his back on them.

Klag knew very little about the Trakliv system. He did know that it was a blue giant with only a few asteroids around it. He saw none of that; instead a huge, roiling mass of energy filled the screen. "How big is that?"

"I cannot get a precise reading, sir," the ensign at operations said, "but it has engulfed the *entire* system."

"Analyze it."

"I cannot, sir."

Klag stood and whirled around to face the ensign. "Explain."

"Sir, sensors do not read it."

The gunner and pilot both verified that at Klag's request, which was the only reason why the operations officer continued to live.

Retaking his seat, Klag said, "Search for the Kinshaya vessel."

"Captain," the pilot said, "the warp trail leads directly into . . . into *that*." She pointed at the viewer. "There's no sign of it otherwise."

Klag cursed. Whatever this anomaly was, it may have consumed not only the Trakliv system, but their prey as well. *We have been denied our honor and our revenge.*

"Continue scanning," he said with a snarl. "I want the Kinshaya found and that anomaly explained!"

THIRD INTERLUDE

———————◆———————

The Continuum

Ten years before the end of the universe

"THERE IS A PROBLEM," Q SAID, "AND YOU'RE BEST equipped to handle it."

He couldn't help but laugh at that. "Oh, *now* I'm well equipped to handle things, am I?" The summons from the Continuum had taken him away from his and Vash's trip through the galaxy. Not that Vash was all that put out by his departure. In fact, she seemed downright grateful. In all honesty, he had half a mind just to leave her to her own devices, the silly cow.

"*Certain* things, yes," Q said with a sigh.

Q batted her eyelashes at him. "One or two, at least."

"You are the closest we have to an expert on humanity," Q said. "Q has already argued eloquently for your reinstatement into the Continuum," Q added, indicating Q—who had indeed reversed his position, going from getting him tossed out to letting him back in. "But it is despite your endless fascination with humans, not because of it."

He didn't believe that for a second. They were coming around to his point of view, they just weren't willing to admit it!

"That fascination is actually kinda useful," Q said, taking over. "Remember Q and Q?"

Of course he remembered them. How could he forget the two who had actually gone to Earth and taken on human form? But they were dead and gone, having been unable to resist the temptation to use their powers. What did they have to do with anything?

Unless . . . He remembered that Q and Q had reproduced, and he remembered the speed at which humans aged. "Their offspring."

"She is becoming aware of her powers, as a legacy of the Q. She must be taught and brought back to the Continuum—or eliminated. We cannot have the Q contaminated with mortality."

He agreed wholeheartedly. "I'll get on it right away." He sought her out and then burst out laughing. "Oh, this is *wonderful*!"

Q and Q both sighed. "Yes, we thought you of all people would find her location amusing."

"Worry not, my fellow Q—I know that I can

count on Jean-Luc and his band of merry men." He chuckled at his own joke; the last time he visited the *Enterprise,* he'd sent them to that Sherwood Forest fantasyland. "They can be trusted to help me out."

Q raised her eyebrow. "After all you've done to them in the past, you expect them to help you?"

"Trust me." With that, he departed the Continuum and returned to the *Enterprise.* There was, after all, much to do. For all his joking around, he feared that the time was growing nearer. He had been let back into the Continuum, yes, but the Q were fractured. Some were starting to believe him—Q, of course, was always willing to believe him, even if she didn't always trust him, and Q had come around as well after that business with the *Enterprise* and the Calamarain, but Q and Q and Q were still on the fence, Q and Q and Q and Q were dead set against, and the less said about Q the better.

Best not to wait around any longer. First I'll take care of this proto-Q Jean-Luc has on his ship, then we'll start getting down to brass tacks.

7

---◆---

Enterprise
In orbit of Gorsach IX

One day before the end of the universe

"WE HAD ONE OF THOSE STUPID DEPARTMENT *soirées tonight."* Vicenzo Farrenga's pleasant round face filled the viewscreen in front of Miranda Kadohata, who was smiling with bemusement. Miranda knew that Vicenzo hated those get-togethers. However, Ian Karapips, the chair of Bacco University's linguistics department, thought they "fostered a commonality." Vicenzo opined that the phrase proved Ian had read a Betazoid psychiatric text as a teenager, memorizing it in order to torment future employees.

It was late at night in Lakeside on Cestus III, but ship's time was early morning. Miranda had put the call through to Cestus when she got up and spoke to her husband while she got ready. They were lucky in that they were close enough to the subspace booster relay that there was only a four-second delay in communications with Vicenzo. Other missions might take them too far from any relay station—or be too many sectors away from Cestus—for anything approaching real-time communication, so she wanted to take as much advantage as she could to talk to her husband. Miranda had spent most of the previous night's comm talking with Aoki and making incomprehensible noises at the twins—which was made all the more entertaining by the delay. Now, the time on Cestus meant that all three children were sound asleep.

"How dreadful was it?" Miranda asked, using the four-second delay to put her uniform jacket on.

Vicenzo ran his hands through his thick, dark hair. He was constantly adjusting his hair, even though it was always perfect, as far as Miranda was concerned. Finally, he said, *"Not as bad as it could've been, really, but we've got Aoki to thank for that."*

That surprised Miranda. "Aoki was there?"

Vicenzo, however, was still talking. *"Well, Aoki and the others. Ian encouraged those of us with children to bring them along—and yeah, she was there, I'm explaining that,"* he added as her words finally arrived. *"So Esmeralda, Bridget, and Jenni all brought their kids, and they were out playing on Ian's porch. Before you ask,"* he said quickly, *"I got Dorian to watch the twins. I'm fine with a five-year-old 'fostering commonalities,' but there was no reason for the twins to suffer through it."*

Miranda smiled. Aoki loved "going out" and neither of her parents could stop her once she heard the word "out." Aoki knew how to spell it in seven languages. Miranda was relieved that Vicenzo was leaving the house when he wasn't teaching, and trusting Dorian to watch Colin and Sylvana. He had requested a lightened workload at the university— only two classes, which met only once a week each—for the year, so he could spend more time with the twins.

"So anyhow," Vicenzo went on, *"we had a decent dinner and spent the whole time gossiping about all the other departments—y'know, like usual—and the kids are out playing on Ian's porch. I say 'I want some air,' but mostly I wanna check on 'em, y'know? So just as I go out, they all scream and run into one corner of the porch. I check, and there's this little* greelak *poking its head out from between two of the porch slats."*

Miranda nodded, even though Vicenzo wouldn't see her do that for four seconds. A *greelak* was a lizardlike creature native to Cestus III, with seven legs—two in the back, two in the middle, two under the shoulder, and one under the neck— bright red scales, and rather than teeth had a shelf of enamel that looked nastier than it actually was, considering that *greelaks* were herbivores. They rarely grew more than ten centimeters long and were mostly harmless.

"The little guy's just looking out, and the kids are all cowering and screaming, so I pick him up and hold him in my hand. I start telling 'em that they're harmless and all that stuff and that there's nothing to be afraid of. After about a minute of that—and, y'know, of holding the little guy in my hand, showing *he's harmless—they start to inch outta the corner. Aoki's the first one to do that, and the rest of 'em follow suit."* Vicenzo grinned. *"Now here's the good part. First, Aoki says, 'See, grown-ups know stuff!'"*

Miranda grinned right back, picturing her little girl standing up straight, nodding her head emphatically, and saying those words.

"Then Esmeralda comes out, sees the greelak *in my hand, screams, and runs into another corner of the porch."*

At that, Miranda couldn't help but burst out laughing. "Oh, that's *wonderful.*"

"So then our little girl rolls her eyes, stares at Esmeralda—yeah, it is wonderful, isn't it? Anyhow, Aoki stares at Esmeralda and says, 'Don't you know anything? Greelaks are harmless!'"

Her laughter continuing, Miranda bit back a reply, not wanting to fall victim to the delay. After a couple of seconds, during which she started to tie her long dark hair into a bun in the back, she realized that Vicenzo was done. "Thank you for that, my love, that's wonderful. No doubt the high point of the evening."

Four seconds, then: *"Well, no commonalities got fostered, that's for damn sure. So how're things there? Every time we talk, I go on about the twins or Aoki or the university. You haven't said anything about the* Enterprise. *How is it? What're the people like? Is it like it was when you were there before?"*

She sat in front of the viewer. "Well, technically, love, it's not the same ship. And half the command crew's gone. But it's the same in some ways, certainly. Beverly's still wonderful, and Geordi's still a delight—though he seemed a bit off at dinner last night. I've spoken to the new counselor a few times, and she's quite good at her job—though I'm told she was at loggerheads with the captain during that Borg nonsense they went through. And the new security chief is a bit of a wanker, truth be told." She started tapping her chin with her right index finger, a nervous habit she'd picked up years ago. "Then there's the captain and Worf. They're both exactly the same as they were twelve years ago when I left the D, and yet both completely different. The captain still radiates that incredible *presence,* but he also seems a lot more relaxed. Worf's still as much a Klingon warrior but somehow not quite as scary to a commander as he was to a lieutenant. It's odd, both of them are always the focal point of whatever room they're in at a given moment. At dinner last night, Worf actually *smiled.* Twelve years ago, I was near convinced that a smile would crack his face in half. I understand he was married for about a year when he was posted on that station near Bajor—that probably mellowed him some."

She saw Vicenzo chuckle, no doubt in reaction to the face-cracking-in-half line. Then, four seconds after she finished, he asked, *"Yeah, but what's the ship like? You fitting in okay as second officer?"*

"So far. Honestly, it's only been nine days of flying at warp eight to Gorsach. Not exactly what you'd call high-maintenance duty."

"You seem to be enjoying it so far. I haven't seen you this giddy in ages."

"Oh, I am, believe me," she said with a smile. "This is the assignment of a lifetime. I wish I was serving with Data as my first . . ."

"I'm glad I at least got to meet him that one time."

"So'm I." She laughed. "That was quite a dinner, wasn't it? I still can't believe Data actually answered every single one of Aoki's questions—and answered them in a way she'd understand too." Vicenzo and Aoki had traveled to Earth to visit Miranda at Starfleet Command, where she'd been assigned, and Data had joined them for dinner. Data had said that Aoki had reminded him fondly of a young boy named Artim who had taught him a great deal about being a child.

"In any case, this morning's my first away team, so—" Suddenly, Miranda pursed her lips and blinked a few times. "Oh, bollocks. Computer, what time is it?"

"The time is zero-six fifty-five hours."

She cursed to herself. After going to all the trouble of waking up an hour early, she'd completely lost track of time and now had to leave immediately.

"I'm running late, love, I have to go! I love you."

She waited the four seconds, and then he said, *"I love you, too. Go! Seek out new life and stuff."*

After ending the transmission, she sprinted toward the doors. Just as they parted, she remembered she needed her tricorder, ran back inside, couldn't remember where she'd put it, recalled finally that it was on the desk in the other room, grabbed it, dashed out of her quarters toward the turbolift, almost knocking over some poor ensign on the way. Miranda had already loaded the tricorder with all the information she'd need for the survey, including everything she'd had for the meeting the previous night.

The doors opened on her approach, thank all the gods and fates in the known universe. As Kadohata ran in, she said, "Transporter Room—" She panicked again, suddenly not remembering which room it was. Then it came to her. "Three!" *Bloody hell, woman, get your brain together. You're the second officer now.*

The lift moved at what seemed to Miranda to be a snail's pace. She tapped her combadge and said, "Computer, please download current reading from Gorsach IV and V."

"Affirmative, downloaded."

Miranda nodded. "Bravo." She checked her

tricorder, scrolling through the data, pushing to the front anything she thought she could use on the surface. "Time?"

"The time is zero-six fifty-nine hours."

When the lift finally arrived, Miranda dashed through the doors, barely giving them time to part, and jogged to the transporter room.

Of course, Worf and Leybenzon were already there. Leybenzon looked somewhat cheesed off, what Miranda now assumed was his natural state. She was right on time.

Worf said, "Let us proceed." He stepped up onto the transporter platform. Leybenzon handed Miranda her phaser weapon, which she holstered. Both she and Leybenzon joined Worf on the platform.

To Ensign Luptowski, who was standing behind the controls, Worf ordered, "Energize."

The transporter room grew indistinct, fading into a silvery shimmer, then immediately coalescing into a large expanse of brownish-red rock, broken by numerous trees and bushes. The rock curved upward about fifty meters ahead of them. Turning around as she materialized, Kadohata saw that the rock curved upward at the same distance all around—they were at the canyon's epicenter.

The commander blinked in surprise. The canyon had scanned as circular on long-range, but she hadn't realized it was such a *perfect* circle. Pulling out her tricorder, she opened it and had it link with the sensor data the *Enterprise* had acquired since coming into orbit. Jill Rosado had done a full sensor sweep, starting with the away team's position and continuing outward. She'd gotten basic readings on the entire planet before the beaming down.

Leybenzon also had his tricorder out in one hand and his phaser in another. *Typical,* Miranda thought. The security chief said, "I'm reading no structures of any kind, and no energy emissions, except for the planet's magnetic field." Nodding, Leybenzon put away the tricorder. "No life signs, either, sir. We're alone down here." Despite this, Miranda noted that he kept the phaser out.

Leybenzon's tactical scan matched what the ship had picked up and what Miranda was reading now. She couldn't really blame Leybenzon for verifying, but Miranda still found his attitude a little too gung-ho.

However, she had more pressing concerns. What she had thought to be an anomaly, or an artifact of the less specific nature of long-range sensors, had turned out to be something a bit more serious. "Commander?" she said to Worf.

"Report," the first officer ordered.

"Something very . . . very odd, sir." Kadohata scanned the canyon once more. "This canyon is perfectly circular. The diameter is a hundred-seven-point-eight meters all 'round. The upcurve of the rocks is *exactly* fifty-three-point-nine meters from the center of our beamdown point in every direction. On top of that, there are three cave entrances, all spaced *precisely* forty-two-point-six meters apart."

"Unusual," Worf observed.

"It's not just that. From the long-range, I noticed that the planet seemed to be a little *too* perfectly aligned. I thought it was just because we weren't getting the complete picture, but I was wrong. I'm reading deposits of topaline and dilithium, but they're precisely evenly distributed."

Leybenzon shrugged. "So?"

"Dilithium tends to come in bunches, and it also tends to be buried fairly deep, but this is all over everywhere. And topaline is *always* concentrated in single areas. But not here."

Worf said, "We have encountered unusual dilithium deposits in the past."

Miranda nodded. "Yes, but the Selcundi Drema dilithium deposits were still within the range of expected distribution—the far range, admittedly. This is nowhere near. And it's not just that." She pointed at the plants, and also at one of the insects that flitted about. "Those trees, those bushes, that fly—they're all symmetrical."

Again, Leybenzon said, "So? *We're* symmetrical."

"Not completely." She looked at the security chief. "Your left eye is slightly above your right. My left thumb's a bit shorter than the right one, and one of my breasts is larger than the other."

"I don't see how any of this matters," Leybenzon said dismissively.

That's because you're not listening. "There's more. I'm detecting no signs of bacteria or blight.

All the leaves on the trees are perfectly healthy. I'm picking up a fruit tree at the top of the canyon, and all the fruits are ripe, with no blemishes or bruises." She sighed. "Look, this never happens. Perfection does not occur in nature."

Nodding, Worf said, "It happens only by design."

"Precisely."

Leybenzon frowned. "Okay. So you're saying someone constructed this place?"

Miranda shrugged. "It's the only conclusion that makes sense. And it's not like there isn't precedent. There's Beta Omicron Delta III, an amusement park planet where everything was completely artificial. There's Talos IV, where the natives cast illusions so sophisticated that early Starfleet instruments were fooled. There's Ydriej, where they completely rebuilt their society with photonic energy—basically turning their entire planet into a holodeck." At Worf's slightly surprised look, Miranda added, "When we got the long-range readings, I did a bit of spelunking into the records. I was fairly sure it was a false alarm, but I wanted to be prepared just in case."

"Admirable," Worf said.

"Sir, I recommend we beam up immediately." Leybenzon now sounded tense, having thought through the consequences of what Miranda was saying. *Or perhaps,* she thought with bemusement, *he's recalling that there used to be a death penalty attached to visiting Talos IV.*

"No," Worf said after considering for a moment.

"At least not yet." He tapped his combadge. "Worf to *Enterprise*."

"Picard here. Go ahead, Number One."

Worf almost flinched. "Number One" had been the captain's designation for William Riker for a decade and a half, and the Klingon was still not accustomed to it being used for him. However, Miranda knew that it had also been what Captain Picard had called his first officer on the *Stargazer*.

"Captain," he finally said, "Commander Kadohata has detected some disturbing readings."

At a nod from Worf, Miranda proceeded to repeat her report, albeit in more condensed fashion.

"How do you intend to proceed, Number One?"

"We will continue to investigate the canyon. Recommend that Ensign Luptowski acquire a hard transporter lock on the away team."

"Agreed. Picard to Luptowski."

"Go ahead, sir," said the ensign's high-pitched voice.

"Maintain a hard lock on the away team and stand by to beam them up at the slightest sign of trouble— particularly if the lock wavers in any way. I'd rather err on the side of beaming them up without cause."

"Understood, Captain."

"Thank you, sir," Worf said. "We will now proceed to investigate the caverns."

"Very well. Keep this channel open."

"Aye, sir." Worf looked at Miranda. "Do you have a recommendation as to which cavern to investigate first, Commander?"

Kadohata peered down at her tricorder again. Unfortunately, it wasn't forthcoming with much by way of answers. She shrugged. "One's as good as another, to be honest. They've each got topaline and dilithium both, and—"

"Both?" Leybenzon asked. "That is unusual, if not outright impossible."

"Yes, Lieutenant, thank you." Miranda wished she could have taken the snappish tone back, but Leybenzon didn't seem put out by the rebuke. "In any event, we might as well go with that one." She pointed at the one that was in front of the direction she happened to be facing.

"Very well," Worf said, and started walking toward the cavern.

Leybenzon stepped into his path. "Sir, I recommend I take the lead."

Worf opened his mouth to speak, but stopped. Miranda figured his instincts were still that of the chief of security, but that was Leybenzon's task now. "Of course, Lieutenant. Take point. I will bring up the rear."

They walked at a brisk pace, Leybenzon keeping his phaser in front of him. Miranda asked, "Are you sure that's necessary, Lieutenant? There's no one and nothing around—aside from the bugs," she added as she brushed her free hand at a perfectly symmetrical insect that was buzzing around her nose.

"I would rather have it out and not need it than the other way around," Leybenzon said without looking at her. He was too busy regarding the path in front of him. Miranda noticed that his head never stayed still.

Shrugging, Kadohata turned back to her tricorder, which wasn't telling her anything different. Within fifteen minutes, they'd reached the mouth of the first cavern.

Two hours later, having thoroughly inspected two of the three caverns, they turned their attention to the final one. As with the first two, it was a cave about thirty meters deep, the cavern curved and twisty, in the exact same pattern. The concentration of dilithium and topaline remained constant, and in the same places as the first two.

This has got to be the dullest away team I've ever been assigned to, Miranda thought dolefully.

Less than ten meters into the final cave, Leybenzon stopped.

Miranda almost didn't notice and came within a hairsbreadth of bumping into him. "What is it?" she asked.

"I—" Leybenzon hesitated, sounding far less confident than Miranda had ever heard him sound in her brief association with him. "I do not . . . understand."

"What is wrong, Lieutenant?" Worf asked.

"I cannot move." He backed up. "Let me amend that—I cannot move *forward.* Something is stopping me."

Miranda held up her tricorder. "I'm not reading anything different here. Certainly nothing that would indicate this." She walked past Leybenzon and then stopped. Blinking, she tried to move forward, but her legs suddenly stopped obeying her brain's commands. "All right, then. This is . . . odd."

"Report, Number One," came Picard's voice from all of their combadges.

"There is some force preventing us from advancing all the way into the final cavern, Captain." As Worf spoke, he stepped forward, his own tricorder out, and didn't get any farther ahead than Miranda had. "We are detecting no cause for this—no barrier, no force field, no indications of telepathic or telekinetic energies."

Miranda admonished herself for not checking, especially since she was the one who brought up Talos IV, which was probably what put the notion in Worf's mind. *That's why he's the first.*

Leybenzon started, "I believe—" when they were all distracted by the sound of snarling.

Whirling around, Miranda saw four quadrupeds standing in the mouth of the cavern. They were each about three meters long, covered in short, spiky black fur, a long snout, a two-pointed barbed horn sticking out of their forehead, and claws that looked like those of a wolverine.

"There's no sign—" Miranda started, then noticed that *now* her tricorder was reading the creatures.

The two rows of teeth were bared at the landing party, and the creatures were growling very loudly. Miranda knew the look of a predator about to pounce on its prey and immediately used her free hand to unholster her phaser.

However, Worf was saying, *"Enterprise, beam us up, n—"*

The creatures and the cavern dissolved as they re-formed into the transporter room.

"—ow!" Worf holstered his phaser. "Well done, Ensign," he said to Luptowski. Then he tapped his combadge. "Worf to bridge. Landing party has returned to the *Enterprise,* Captain. We are reporting to sickbay."

"I will meet you there, Number One."

Leybenzon faced Worf. "We could have taken down those animals with great ease, Commander. I fail to see—"

"There is no honor in fighting an animal defending its territory, Lieutenant."

Miranda regarded the first officer with surprise. "I thought Klingons valued the hunt."

Worf turned his gaze onto Miranda. "The hunt, yes. But this would not have been a hunt—it would have been a slaughter. And it does not matter. Those animals were not detected by the *Enterprise* or by our tricorders. Neither did they read whatever kept us from going any farther. Something or someone in that cavern is being protected, and we must learn what it is before we engage it."

"We could have done that on the surface," Leybenzon insisted.

"Perhaps—but we will be better armed with more information, and we can obtain that from orbit."

With that, Worf led the way out of the transporter room and toward sickbay.

"Agreed," Leybenzon said, sounding a mite perturbed. "Why are we reporting to *sickbay*?"

"Commander Kadohata mentioned Talos IV. The species native to that world are powerful telepaths who can create sophisticated illusions. It is possible that such beings are present on Gorsach IX, and we are unable to detect them. I wish Doctor Crusher to examine us for evidence of psionic tampering."

Miranda found she couldn't argue with that logic. She tapped her combadge to contact the relief ops officer. "Kadohata to Rosado."

"Go ahead, Commander."

"Jill, I need you to focus the sensors on the cavern we were just beamed out of. Hit it with everything—I want to know the subatomic makeup of the dirt on the floor."

"I'll get right on it, sir."

Worf gave Miranda a nod of approval as they entered the turbolift. "Sickbay," the first officer's powerful voice filled the lift as the doors closed.

Having left T'Lana in charge of the bridge, Picard proceeded immediately to sickbay; the captain was concerned. This was supposed to be a simple mission, one where the crew could revel in the exploration of a new world, but now there were complications.

A constructed world. In truth, this raised several fascinating possibilities, but Picard was concerned about whoever it was behind the proverbial curtain. While the landing party explored the caverns,

Picard had called up previous Starfleet missions that had planets that were constructed, whether physically, holographically, or telepathically. Each, it seemed, ended badly.

The captain entered sickbay to see Doctor Crusher passing a medical scanner over Kadohata, while Doctor Tropp was doing the same for Leybenzon. A medtech with his back to Picard was fussing over an equipment cart.

Worf was standing next to Nurse Ojibwa. He turned to face Picard when he entered. "I felt it prudent to report to sickbay to determine if there was any evidence of telepathic tampering."

Picard nodded. "A wise precaution. Doctor?"

Having finished the second officer's exam, Crusher shook her head. "Worf checked out okay, and I'm not seeing anything on Miranda to indicate the kind of telepathic tampering the commander was concerned about. Having said that, each telepathic species we know leaves a different imprint upon the brain. Betazoid telepathy shows heightened activity in the hippocampus, whereas a Vulcan mind-meld shows an increase in neurotransmitters to the—"

Holding up a hand, Picard said, "Doctor, what does this all mean?"

Crusher continued, "What it boils down to is that neither Worf nor Miranda shows any signs of invasive telepathy *that we're aware of.*"

Tropp set down his medical scanner. "And neither does Lieutenant Leybenzon."

Leybenzon sat up. "And yet there was *something*

that prevented us from moving deeper into that cavern."

Kadohata added, "Yeah, something that literally set wolves at us."

"Obviously," Worf said, "someone does not wish us on that planet, sir—or at the very least, not in that cavern."

"Oh, you don't know the half of it, microbrain."

No. Picard felt his stomach sink down into his toes. His heart rate probably tripled at the sound of that voice. It belonged to the trickster who had been tormenting him—and his crew, but mostly him, it seemed—on and off since the *Enterprise*-D's very first mission.

Glancing over his shoulder, Picard saw that the medtech had turned around to reveal dark hair, a smug smile, mischievous eyes, and an all-around irritating demeanor.

Picard felt the blood drain from his face, and he could feel Worf tense next to him without even having to look.

"Hello, Jean-Luc, sorry I've been away so long. I must say, I just *love* what you've done with the place. Hope you did up the guest room for me."

Sighing, Picard said, "Q."

FOURTH INTERLUDE

———◆———

The Continuum

Ten years before the end of the universe

HE WAS CONVINCED THAT THE REST OF THE CON-
tinuum was wrong. In fact, most of the evidence
he had favored the opposite conclusion—but try
telling the Continuum that. *A bunch of hidebound
old toads, most of them.* It had seemed at first that
they were starting to believe him, but believing him
meant taking action, and the Q were never especially skilled at taking action.

Q, at least, understood him—or, rather, she toler-
ated him, and had for many millennia now, despite
his excesses.

This, however, was not one of those excesses.
Not this time. All right, perhaps he was going about

it all in a way that was excessive, but that was where the fun was.

After that business with Q—or, rather, "Amanda Rogers," as she rather insanely insisted upon calling herself—and the nonsense with Vash, the Continuum had said that they had had enough of humans, that they were more trouble than they were worth, and that he should stay away from them.

He pleaded. He begged. He cajoled.

Did they listen? Of course not. They never ever ever listened to him. It grew tiresome. Instead, they threw ridiculous tasks at him, tried to get him to become a good and proper Q. And, to an extent, he obeyed. After all, he'd been cast out once over humanity and was in no great rush to relive the experience. Being human on Jean-Luc's toy ship was quite probably the worst ordeal of his life, mostly by virtue of it being the *only* ordeal in his life. He was damned if he'd do *that* again.

So on the surface he continued to do as the Continuum asked.

And behind the scenes, he began to prepare the humans, in particular Jean-Luc. There was much to do with them and precious little time to do it.

Some of the groundwork had already been laid—assuming the humans actually figured it out, though there was no way to know that until the time came—but that still left plenty to do. The first preparation involved Jean-Luc and was the one he intended to have the most fun with. On the brink of death—and wouldn't *that* be a kick in the teeth, Jean-Luc Picard dying before he had a chance to fulfill what he was certain was the captain's destiny—he summoned Jean-Luc to the astral void.

"Welcome to the afterlife, Jean-Luc. You're dead."

8

Imperial *Warbird Valdore*
Romulan Star Empire

One day before the end of the universe

"SHIELDS?" COMMANDER DONATRA SCREAMED OVER the din of the battle klaxon.

From the gunnery station, Centurion T'Relek said, "Down to thirty percent."

Donatra muttered a very old curse that her late lover, Admiral Braeg, used to use. "Where's the rest of the fleet?"

"Unknown, Commander," said Subcommander Liravek, her first officer who also ran the operations console. "Sensors are down."

This time, Donatra yelled the curse. "Are the torpedo systems online yet?"

"Engineering says another minute."

We don't have another minute. She didn't say the words aloud, as it wasn't Liravek's fault that her engineering staff was made up entirely of fools and incompetents. The *Valdore* was still in poor shape, having suffered damage at the hands of Shinzon's *Scimitar,* as well as the rift that had been opened by that vessel's destruction at the hands of the Federation *Starship Enterprise.* Donatra didn't feel comfortable leaving her ship in the hands of the repair crews on the Two Worlds, so she had set course away from Romulus and Remus and toward Artalierh, a shipyard run by someone Donatra knew was loyal to her.

Or, more to the point, not loyal to Tal'Aura.

The former senator had taken over as praetor of the Romulan Star Empire, managing to unite most of the factions that were vying for power in the wake of Shinzon's death. However, Donatra still held sway over a portion of the military—all those under Braeg's command, including those loyal to Donatra and the deceased Commander Suran, plus many who didn't enjoy Tal'Aura's leadership. Tal'Aura's hold on the praetor's chair was tenuous. If she wanted to remain praetor, Tal'Aura would need Donatra's support.

Donatra had supported Shinzon only because Braeg did, and she had quickly realized that her mentor had been mistaken. They had thought that a

Reman—or a human raised as a Reman—would be more pliable. The senate had grown weaker with each idiot that ascended from its ranks, to the praetorship, culminating in that great fool Hiren. Donatra did not mourn Hiren's death, nor the deaths of the rest of the senate at the hands of Tal'Aura. However, Donatra believed that the empire would be a better place if Tal'Aura had been sealed in the senate chambers with her bomb.

Did Tal'Aura order this attack on Donatra? The commander had no idea. Under normal circumstances, *Valdore,* one of the top-of-the-line *Mogai*-class warbirds, should be able to make short work of the four birds-of-prey currently harassing them. Two of the birds-of-prey—one of which was now destroyed—knew where their shields were weakest and had concentrated their fire there.

Which is why I don't have sensors or weapons, and the shields are draining away. The attack was so sudden that *Valdore* lost sensors before Liravek had been able to get a positive ID on the ships. Obviously, there was a spy on board, whose throat Donatra would happily slit when this was all over. *Assuming I make it out alive.*

No, she thought angrily, *I will make it out alive. I have not come this far to fail now.*

"Sensors are back online," Liravek said. "We're identifying the three birds-of-prey as *Elieth, Arest,* and *Esemar.*" The destroyed vessel was the *Lallasthe.*

Nodding, Donatra said, "Good." Commander Horrhae was master of this squadron, and *Lallasthe* was her flagship. The others continued the fight out of a sense of loyalty to her or her orders. *Perhaps they can be convinced.*

Liravek smiled when he reported. "*Dominus, Rohallhik,* and *Intrakhu* are en route at warp seven and will arrive in fifteen minutes."

"Torpedo launchers back online," T'Relek added. "Still no disruptors, but we can fire back."

"Load bays," Donatra said, "and open a channel to—" She thought quickly, trying to remember Horrhae's three subcommanders, finally settling on the seniormost, and therefore the one most likely to listen to reason. "—Subcommander Norvid on *Elieth.*"

"Yes, Commander," Liravek said.

"We have nothing to say to you, traitress," Norvid said without preamble. She did not do Donatra the courtesy of showing her face on the viewer.

"I'm not the traitress, Norvid. Horrhae was for firing on an Imperial warbird. She has paid for that mistake with her life—don't make the same mistake. Three more *Mogai*-class vessels will arrive shortly. If you survive the encounter, you will be brought up on charges and likely executed."

"Our orders came from the praetor." Norvid, however, sounded much less sure of herself.

"Did they? How do you know this? Did you see the order? Do you truly imagine that any praetor worth her salt would order you to fire on a loyal soldier of the empire?"

"You supported the usurper."

"So did the praetor. We were all fooled by that

Reman trickster, but he has already paid for that folly. You should not make the same mistake." She leaned forward in her chair—*Valdore* was transmitting visual even if *Elieth* wasn't. "You command this fleet now, Norvid. Will you lead them to victory or disgrace?"

There was a lengthy pause.

Liravek then said, "All three birds-of-prey are standing down weapons, Commander."

Thank the Elements. "You've made the right choice, Norvid."

"I've made no choice yet, Commander. You are bound for Artalierh, yes?"

Another fact that was not well-known but obviously transmitted to Horrhae's fleet by a spy on *Valdore.* "That is our destination."

"Good. Our communications systems are not strong enough for real-time communication with the Two Worlds from here, but Artalierh has communication amplifiers and relays that allow such. We will escort you there and determine the source of the commander's orders."

Donatra wondered, *And what happens when the truth of the orders comes out?* She suspected that, even if Tal'Aura or one of her lackeys had been responsible, Donatra's having survived the attack would cause the praetor to deny giving the order, especially with the convenient scapegoat of the deceased Commander Horrhae. *If she does deny it, I can then count on Norvid's support.* Donatra smiled. Every little bit helped, after all.

"I agree to your terms, Subcommander. We will proceed as soon as *my* other vessels arrive." Donatra made sure to emphasize the possessive pronoun. These weren't just other ships of the same class; these were vessels whose commanders had sworn fealty to Donatra. It didn't hurt to remind Norvid of that.

"Commander!" Liravek's voice sounded strained.

Not happy at the interruption, especially while the channel to *Elieth* was still open, Donatra said, "What is it, Subcommander?" She placed enough emphasis on Liravek's rank to remind him that she had promoted him recently, and what Donatra had bestowed she could also take away.

"The other ships in the fleet—Commander, they're *gone!*"

Donatra stood up. "They haven't cloaked?"

"No, Commander—and we're detecting something where the ships were."

"Put it on the viewer."

Liravek did so, and what Donatra saw was eerily familiar yet different. It reminded her all too much of the roiling energy that was left in the wake of the *Scimitar*'s destruction. Her people had dubbed it the "Great Bloom," though Donatra preferred to think of it as Shinzon's Folly. Or, perhaps, Romulus's Folly, given that it was those left behind who were paying for Shinzon's actions.

This, however, was more chaotic even than the Bloom. "Analysis," she said.

Shaking his head, Liravek said, "I can provide

none, Commander. Sensors cannot penetrate the object. We know it's there only because we *see* it."

Turning toward Liravek's station to her left, Donatra said, "That's impossible."

"And yet, Commander, it is true."

"My science officer is telling me the same, Commander," Norvid reported. *"We see this strange energy, but we cannot detect it. It does, however, appear to be growing."*

Looking back at the viewer, Donatra saw that the phenomenon was indeed getting larger.

"It would seem," she said slowly, "that we have more than one thing to report to Romulus when we arrive at Artalierh."

"Indeed," Norvid said. *"I suggest we leave immediately."*

Donatra looked at the pilot, a young decurion who had been promoted up from engineering last week. "Set course for Artalierh and execute immediately."

"Yes, Commander."

FIFTH INTERLUDE

The Continuum

Six years before the end of the universe

HE SAT WITH Q AND THEIR SON, Q, AND HE HAD TO admit to reveling in the child's company. Having a son had been a means to an end at first, a way to curtail the civil war that had erupted in the formerly complacent Continuum.

It had all been the philosopher's fault. Well, to be honest, it had been the humans' fault. Somehow, they'd found their way into what they referred to as the Delta Quadrant and then stumbled onto the philosopher's prison. Worse, they *freed* him.

He went to deal with it, of course, as the Continuum instructed. He was the Continuum's dutiful little boy now, cleaning up all their messes. First

Trelane, now the philosopher. It grew tiresome.

But he did as he was told, biding his time. When he could, he continued to prepare Jean-Luc and the others. He had lied to Jean-Luc—hardly the first time—and told him that the anti-time test was administered by the entire Continuum. But then, Jean-Luc had always believed him, from the very start.

All things being equal, of course, he would have let the philosopher kill himself, if for no other reason than it would shake the Continuum to its very core. And indeed, after the philosopher claimed asylum on Kathy Janeway's little lost ship, he was more than happy to let the philosopher's Vulcan advocate argue the case for suicide. For appearance's sake—the Continuum was always watching—he continued to defend the Continuum's position, but he was secretly grateful for the final verdict Kathy gave.

He supposed he could have shown his gratitude by sending *Voyager* back home, but he knew what lay ahead for them. Kathy's little band of starlost simpletons would do much to curtail the Borg's activities in what humans called the Alpha Quadrant, which was, he thought, necessary. *If the Borg discovered Them . . .* He shuddered. That was why he had sent the *Enterprise* to meet them in the first place a few moments ago.

However, his desire to shake the Continuum out of its complacence worked a little too well. The philosopher's death split the Continuum in two, fracturing them more than his arguments about humanity ever could. Q—who had stymied him from the very start—led the other side in the civil war, even condemning him to a firing squad at one point. Q, though, came to his rescue, as she often did. Having already recruited a Vulcan physician to train the Q in how to heal themselves—never before had the omnipotent beings been injured—Q then brought the tattooed stiff, the philosopher's Vulcan advocate, and the comedy stylings of Kim and Paris into the Continuum to rescue him and Kathy.

Kathy had been present because, thinking that an injection of literal new blood into the Continuum was what was needed, he had tried to convince her to have a baby with him. (She was the best available choice of the human women Q knew. Vash was too irresponsible to make a good mother, which was what made her appealing in the first place, but not for this. And if he propositioned Crusher or Troi on the *Enterprise,* it would just get Jean-Luc's and Riker's backs up.) When it was all over, Kathy instead suggested he mate with Q.

That did the trick. The Continuum stopped fighting itself, and the universe was a safer place.

He had to admit to enjoying fatherhood. They had several adventures together—the Great Barrier, the gateways, the Bolgar. He told q several wonderful stories, even bringing them together into an end-of-the-universe narrative that he was quite proud of, and he tried to teach q about the universe. Meanwhile, he had a little fun on his own with those kids on Liten, and he continued to run errands for the Continuum, like that business with the Nacene. When q got to be so much that even his mother couldn't deal with him, he fobbed q off on Kathy, which worked rather well. (He was also delighted to see that Kathy had actually tamed several Borg, something that had to irk the Collective, and probably would keep them away from Them, thus reassuring him that leaving Kathy and the gang stuck in exile was the right thing to do.)

Then the fateful day came at last. Jean-Luc's little ship was on its way to Gorsach IX. Leaving q with Q (who had finally been convinced to come back and help raise the little monster after he'd calmed down on Kathy's ship), he hied his way back to the *Enterprise*.

9

———

Enterprise
In orbit of Gorsach IX

One day before the end of the universe

"AH, JEAN-LUC, IT'S *SO* GOOD TO SEE YOU AGAIN. I know I've been much more dilatory in my visits since you upgraded to this deboned chicken of a ship, but I've been fairly busy. After all, I'm a family man now."

Picard sighed. He supposed he should have realized. "I take it that Gorsach IX is your doing, Q?"

Q snapped his fingers, the medtech uniform changing to that of a Starfleet captain with a flash of light. Now that he was no longer disguised, it was typical of Q to go back to his default of appearing in a Starfleet captain's uniform. Just once, Picard wished Q would change his shtick.

"Sorry, Jean-Luc, but no. For once, I'm simply a passive observer."

"I find that impossible to believe, Q."

Q rolled his eyes. "Of course you do, Jean-Luc. You never believe a word I say, certainly when it involves something you cannot possibly comprehend." He started to pace around sickbay. "I must admit, not coming back until now was a somewhat deliberate choice on my part. Riker and Troi are gone, for one thing—this means I'm spared the possibility of Troi's mother being present. As for Riker, insulting him was becoming rather like shooting fish in a barrel. I do get bored *so* easily."

"And yet you keep coming back," Crusher said tightly.

"What can I say, Doctor, I'm a sucker for comic opera."

"Enough!" Picard said. "Q, either ex—"

"'—plain yourself,'" Q interrupted, doing what Picard grudgingly admitted was a passable impersonation of the captain's own tone of voice, "'or get the hell off my ship!' Yes, yes, yes, Jean-Luc, I've heard it all before, and I've always ignored it, so may we please dispense with the usual shouting and get on with the business at hand?" Without waiting for an answer, Q turned to Worf. "So I see Picard made you first officer." He shrugged. "Well, Riker proved that any idiot can do the job, though I must admit, microbrain, I never thought of you as just *any* idiot."

Worf, who had folded his arms over his chest, simply stared impassively at Q.

"What, no growl? No threats? No forward motions designed to unconvincingly intimidate?"

"No," was all Worf said, remaining rigid.

Q nodded approvingly. "Progress. You'll be walking without dragging your knuckles next." Then he turned to face the biobeds. "Newbies! So nice to see some fresh faces 'round these parts. Good riddance to Riker and Troi, of course, but Data is sorely missed. How fitting that he ended a life spent in pursuit of becoming more human in an idiotic gesture worthy of the lowliest human."

Seeing that Leybenzon was starting to move off his biobed, Picard started to speak, but Worf beat him to it. "Lieutenant! At ease."

His entire body tensed so tightly that Picard feared he would snap in two.

Leybenzon protested, "But, sir—"

Q leaned toward Leybenzon. "Best listen to microbrain, chuckles." He turned to Picard. "What is it with you and security chiefs, anyhow? You go through them the way Kathy goes through hairstyles, from Tasha all the way down to this lout."

Every instinct in Picard screamed *do something,* but his intellect reminded him that it was completely pointless because there was nothing he *could* do, except make an ass of himself. The years had taught him that Q did what he did, and there wasn't a thing Picard or Worf or Leybenzon or anyone could do about it. The best approach was to wait him out and let him play his silly games until he filled them in on his true purpose.

His hand going to his phaser, Leybenzon said, "Captain, Commander—I cannot simply stand here and—"

"And do *what*?" Q asked in a low, dangerous voice.

"Get frozen, most like." That was Kadohata, who had gotten up from her biobed. "That's what happened when he first came on board. Froze the conn officer, a nice young chap name of Ricardo Torres. He was a friend of mine."

Turning to Kadohata, Q said, "Ah, the Tinker-toy's replacement. And newly procreated too." Q moved to put his arm around Kadohata. "I must say, Randy—do you mind if I call you Randy?"

Kadohata looked at Q's arm like it was a diseased snake but wasn't foolish enough to provoke him. Instead she simply said, "Yes, I do, rather."

"I must say, Randy, I used to think very ill of the entire reproductive process, but since I've fathered a son of my own, I've done a complete one-eighty on the subject. Parenthood is simply wonderful, isn't it?"

"Yes, it is," Kadohata said gamely. "I can't imagine it's the same thing for you, though."

"No. For one thing, I'm actually *raising* my son instead of leaving him at home with the spouse."

Now Kadohata did throw Q's arm off her. "Don't you *dare*! Don't you of all people presume to lecture me!"

"Oh, I wouldn't dream of it, Randy." Q held up his hands. "Pedantic lectures are Jean-Luc's bag, not mine. Besides, at least you've actually *got* progeny. The doctor's spawn went cosmic—a decent choice, though I've always found the Travelers rather dull—and the big bad Worf over there has his little failure, but the rest of them . . ."

Worf still had his arms folded. Picard was grateful to see his total lack of reaction, except a touch of pride as he said, "Alexander is the Federation ambassador to the Klingon Empire."

"Yes, well, they had to have someone in there to make your tenure in the position look good." He turned to Tropp. "And another physician, subjecting himself to the whims of Doctor Crusher. Let's hope he doesn't turn out like Selar did."

Picard finally asked, "Q, what is your business here?"

Q seemed surprised. "What? Isn't it enough that I want to visit my old pals on the *Enterprise*?"

"No."

Providing a smug smile, Q said, "As usual, Jean-Luc, you see right through me. I do indeed have a purpose here. You see, your mission to Gorsach IX promises to be a major turning point in the life of the universe. And I"—he drew that last syllable out for several seconds, as if trying to create suspense that Picard had no interest in feeling—"want to watch."

"Watch?" Crusher asked dubiously.

"Yes, my dear doctor—and congratulations to

the two of you, by the way. I suspect that sex on a regular basis will do wonders for Jean-Luc's disposition—all I'm here to do is watch."

Resisting commenting on Q's aside, Picard said, "A turning point in the life of the universe? Q, how is an artificial planet involved in something so . . . so large?"

Again, Q rolled his eyes. "Come come, Jean-Luc, you don't expect me to do all the work for you, do you? Part of the fun is watching you dash about and figure it out for yourselves. Unless you're afraid of a few *yrilijk*."

Kadohata asked, "Is that what those creatures were at the cave mouth?"

Q nodded.

"But *yrilijk* are extinct, aren't they?"

Grinning, Q said, "It's a mystery, isn't it? Well, worry not, I'm sure you'll figure it out, you lot always do. Though, of course, one of your starters is on the permanent disabled list, and two have been traded—it remains to be seen if the scrubs on the bench can do the job." Q then waved jauntily. "*Au revoir, mon capitaine.* Remember, I'm just a gas giant's throw away."

And with that, Q disappeared in a flash of light.

Leybenzon frowned. "'Permanent disabled list'?"

"It's a baseball term," Kadohata said, "for players who are too injured to participate in the game, so they go on the list until they're healthy again. It's Q's endearing way of referring to Data. Captain Riker and Commander Troi are the ones who were traded away. You and I, Lieutenant, are the scrubs on the bench."

"Okay." Leybenzon sounded more than a little nonplussed.

Picard turned to Crusher. "Are they cleared to leave sickbay?"

"I don't see why not." Crusher put her medical equipment on a shelf. "Besides, this is probably all Q's doing."

"Indeed," Picard said with a sigh. "Commander Kadohata, Lieutenant Leybenzon, I want every millimeter of Gorsach IX gone over with the *Enterprise* sensors. I want to know everything there is to know about that world before we consider setting foot on it again."

Kadohata said, "Aye, sir."

Leybenzon said, "Sir, with permission, I also wish to do full internal sensor sweeps every ten minutes."

Regarding his security chief doubtfully, Picard said, "Q has never shown up on an internal scan before, Lieutenant."

At that, Leybenzon gave a half smile. "There is a first time for everything, sir."

Worf spoke up. "It would not hurt, Captain."

Nodding, Picard said, "Very well, Lieutenant, make it so." He turned to Worf. "Number One, you have the conn. Meet me in my ready room in twenty minutes. Dismissed." Worf, Kadohata, and Leybenzon all filed quickly out of sickbay.

Picard gave an encouraging look to Crusher

before also departing, headed for their quarters. He had a duty to perform.

Ever since Q first materialized on the bridge of the *Enterprise*-D—in a variety of outdated uniforms and using equally outdated speech patterns—and then interfered with their mission to Farpoint Station, Starfleet had instituted protocols for what to do when Q appeared. First was notification of Command. Most of the protocols were a waste of time. If Q didn't want the *Enterprise*—or whatever ship or starbase or world he might be tormenting—to let Command know he was there, he wouldn't allow the communication to go through. Q could literally do anything he wanted. Q could have rained down destruction on the *Enterprise* many times over, yet the worst he'd actually done was introduce them to the Borg, costing Picard eighteen members of his crew. All of the other deaths the Borg had been responsible for could also be laid at Q's feet. There had been fatalities during the ship's encounters with Q, but none of those were directly Q's fault.

Perhaps, the captain admitted, those eighteen were still so raw because *they* were at the hands of the Borg. At the time, he offered what comfort he could to the families. The families on the *Enterprise* he'd gone to individually. The husband and daughter of Lieutenant Rebekah Grabowski both broke down and cried. The wife of Ensign Franco Garcia took the news with remarkable stoicism. The daughters of Lieutenants Jean-Claude Mbuto and T'Sora shattered a piece of pottery in an emotional display that would have embarrassed their Vulcan mother. The life mate of Ensign Gldrnksrb was so devastated he lapsed into a coma. Over subspace, he spoke with the rest. In particular he remembered the grandparents of Ensign Soon-Tek Han, who had asked if their grandson died doing his duty. Picard said he had. The sad truth was that Han was in the section that the Borg carved out of the *Enterprise* saucer section only because he was late for his shift and was running through the corridor at the time. Seeing the relief on the Hans' faces had been an awkward and bittersweet experience for the captain. Picard had done his duty, knowing full well that to him the words sounded hollow, meaningless.

Their next encounter with the Borg revealed how meaningless his words in fact were. The eighteen weren't dead; they were worse than dead. Their bodies were defiled, their biological distinctness was taken, they were turned into Borg.

In his darkest hours—after Wolf 359—as Counselor Troi slowly worked to heal his broken self, Picard dared to wonder if those eighteen were somehow responsible for Locutus. If their own shining devotion to their captain had not given the Borg the idea to come for him, to use him. Maybe that was the reason Picard remembered each of them so clearly—he knew that he could not fight the Borg and neither could they. And he could not forgive himself for harboring that dark thought.

Picard still firmly believed that Q's point could have been made without sacrificing those lives. But what did the lives of eighteen people matter to an omnipotent being like Q?

That's always the question, isn't it? He keeps coming back here. True, plenty of Starfleet officers—on Deep Space 9, on *Voyager*, on the *Excalibur,* on Luna—had reported sightings of Q over the years, but ultimately he kept coming back to the *Enterprise.* He had a fascination with Picard in particular, having done him the "favor" of showing him what a burden love was and later giving him a far more useful lesson about the value of the choices he made in his misspent youth. Then there was that whole anti-time nonsense, throwing Picard back and forth and back again among three different time frames, none of which actually existed, during which Q admitted to helping Picard beyond the boundaries of the test.

Why us? More to the point, why me?

The captain sighed as he finished sending the communiqué to Starbase 815. Answers would have to wait until Q was good and ready to provide them, a day that, Picard hated to admit, might never come.

He left his quarters and proceeded to the turbolift. The one thing that encouraged Picard was that he had several new crew members to deal with Q. After a while, Q's appearances had become almost routine, in part because everyone knew what to expect. The presence of Kadohata, Leybenzon, and

T'Lana might shake things up. Not that that was necessarily desirable with Q, but Picard would take whatever advantage he could get.

Upon Picard's arrival on the bridge, Worf rose from the command chair. Leybenzon and Kadohata were both working at tactical, Lieutenant Faur manned the conn, and Ensign Mariko Shimura was at ops.

"Planetary scans are continuing," Worf reported. "Estimated completion at zero-four hundred."

Kadohata added, "Lieutenant Leybenzon and I are working on a way to improve the sensor efficiency."

"It is a trick I stole from the Jem'Hadar, actually," Leybenzon said. "The only problem is we have to divert power from some of the science labs—"

"—which I've already authorized," Kadohata said. "I'm sure I'll have some cranky science officers to deal with, but that can come later. With Q around, I want us as efficient as possible."

"Well done, both of you." Picard turned to look at Worf. "My ready room, Number One. Commander Kadohata, you have the conn."

"Aye, sir," Kadohata said, though she remained at tactical with Leybenzon. "Wouldn't it make more sense to increase the bandwidth?"

Leybenzon shook his head even as Picard and Worf headed to the ready room. "That would overload the image translators. We wouldn't be able to see anything."

"Nonsense. If you reroute the—"

Whatever Kadohata planned to reroute was lost

as the door closed behind Worf. Normally Picard would have sat behind his desk, but he found himself feeling restless. Q had that effect on him. So he stood at the port, staring down at this riddle of a planet. Occasionally, he was able to see one or more of the *Enterprise* probes in its orbit.

For his part, Worf stood ramrod straight, arms at his side, looking very much like an Earth redwood.

"The question before us, Number One," Picard said after a silence of several seconds, "is what do we do about Q? The fact that he's here means that there's more to Gorsach IX than meets the eye—which, admittedly, we already knew. Still, his very presence indicates matters of great import."

"To Q, at least," Worf said. "His deeming something important does not make it so."

"True," Picard said with a nod.

"I recommend, sir, that we do nothing."

Picard blinked, then smiled. "I must admit, Worf, that is not a course of action I would have expected you to suggest."

"Perhaps." Worf allowed himself a small smile. "I believe it would be best to ignore Q. Experience has shown us that Q is impossible to defeat by any physical means, so all that leaves us is guile."

"Ignore him and hope he goes away, is that what you're saying, Number One?"

"I doubt we would be so fortunate as that," Worf said dryly. "Q is in many ways like a child who desires attention. Often the best tactic to use against children who so behave is to deny them. The hope is that they will learn that they cannot get noticed simply by demanding it."

"I doubt Q will be any more amenable to a learning experience than he will be to going away," Picard said with another smile. "Still, not playing his game might prompt him to be more forthcoming with specifics as to why Gorsach IX is so critical to him—and to the fate of the universe."

"*If* he is telling the truth about that," Worf said.

Picard considered. "I believe he is, Worf. While Q has often misled us and left out crucial pieces of information, he rarely has baldly lied to us. I believe that this world is important to the universe in some way." He tugged on his uniform jacket. "Continue scanning the surface, Number One. When the planetary scan is complete, have La Forge and Kadohata focus their attention on that cavern. I want a recommendation as to the efficacy of a second away team at zero-nine hundred."

"Aye, sir."

Picard added, "And instruct the crew to ignore Q. No matter the provocation, he is to be treated as if he is not there."

"Gladly, Captain."

As Worf exited the ready room, Picard finally took a seat to record his log. *I just hope this works,* he thought grimly.

T'Lana sat in her office, waiting for her next appointment to arrive. Commander La Forge had already contacted her saying he would be late, due to a crisis in engineering. T'Lana had specifically requested assignment to the *Enterprise* because she had believed that she would be able to do good on this vessel. The recent death of the android Data and its likely effect on Geordi La Forge was one of the areas in which she anticipated her expertise to be of use.

While she waited, T'Lana perused the latest issue of the *Journal of Psychology,* specifically an article by Doctor Chiroka of Bolarus on the subject of the effects of colonization on the group dynamic of Bolians. T'Lana had generally found Chiroka to be a specious theorist, and this article did nothing to change her opinion. T'Lana considered writing a rebuttal.

The doors parted as T'Lana reached the conclusion of the article. Geordi La Forge entered with a smile that humans dubbed "sheepish" for reasons T'Lana had never understood. (She'd seen sheep—they didn't and couldn't smile. Further research led her to believe that it was the timid nature of sheep, and humans' tendency to anthropomorphize animals. However, she was still puzzling over why, since most had never seen a sheep, that arcane term survived.) "Sorry I'm late."

"You have nothing to apologize for. Your presence in engineering was obviously required. This session was at *your* request." T'Lana set down the padd with the journal, not sure whether she'd bother reading the balance of the article. "Please have a seat."

T'Lana had made very few changes to the counselor's office since Deanna Troi's time. The room had bright but not harsh colors that tended to engender a relaxed attitude in most humanoid species. The walls also were capable of changing color to accommodate other species. Blues and reds currently dominated, with two chairs separated by a small table. The chairs were comfortable enough to put the patient at ease, but not so comfortable as to be soporific. The only touches T'Lana had added were to place some Vulcan sculpture on the walls in spots that seemed unnecessarily blank; T'Lana assumed that Counselor Troi had had decorations there but had taken them with her to *Titan*.

La Forge was fidgeting in the chair opposite her, a sign of agitation that T'Lana did not need her years of experience to recognize. Knowing that humans often wanted something to do with their hands in times like that, she asked, "Would you like something to drink, Geordi?"

"No, thanks, I just—" La Forge blew out a breath, expanding his cheeks. "I've been noticing some behavior in myself that I'm not liking all that much."

"What behavior is that?"

"I'm just not . . . comfortable around Miranda Kadohata."

Not surprised by his answer, T'Lana asked, "Why is that?"

That prompted a smile. "I was kinda hoping you could tell me that. It can't just be that she's new. I mean, we get new people on board all the time, and I haven't had problems with any of them. Not even Leybenzon, after last night."

"What occurred last night?"

"In the Riding Club, Leybenzon was holding court with his security people, drinking and telling stories. I joined them after dinner, and it was great. It's weird, he's a *completely* different person off duty." He let out a sigh. "The thing is, until last night, I didn't even *like* Leybenzon. Hell, I'm still not sure if I do or not. But I like Miranda just fine, yet every time she's around . . ."

T'Lana raised an eyebrow as La Forge trailed off. "It is hardly classified information that you were very close friends with Commander Kadohata's predecessor. Some resentment is to be expected."

"It's not that," La Forge said. "I don't resent her at all. She's a good officer, and she's perfect for the job. In fact, she was going to *be* in the job anyhow—Data is supposed to be *first* officer now. If I should be resenting anyone, it's Worf. But . . ."

La Forge trailed off again, prompting T'Lana to ask, "Are you concerned that Commander Kadohata will not perform to Data's standards?"

"No, of course not. Data's the one who picked her, and he wouldn't do that without believing she can do the job."

"That is the second time you have referred to Commander Data in the present tense." T'Lana reached for her padd, wiped the journal from its display, and called up the files she'd had in standby.

Frowning, La Forge said, "I beg your pardon?"

"You said that Data *is* supposed to be first officer now, and that Data *is* the one who picked Commander Kadohata." In truth, La Forge used a contraction the second time that could have been an abbreviation of "Data was," but she wanted to get La Forge to examine his own word choices.

"That's crazy," La Forge said. "Data's dead. He blew up with the *Scimitar.* Hell, I was the last one to see him alive when he left the *Enterprise* for the last time."

"Yes, as you were on"—she looked down at the padd—"stardate 43872."

"That was fourteen years ago," La Forge said, sounding confused. Before T'Lana could explain, he said, "Look, I know that Data's death was horribly unfair and that he should've outlived all of us by several centuries. I also know that if he hadn't done what he did, he'd probably still be dead—and so would the rest of us. Shinzon was about to turn us all into space dust, and Data's the one who kept that from happening. I *know* that. And I saw the *Scimitar* explode with him in it."

"Yes, just as, on stardate 43872, you saw the *Shuttlecraft Pike* explode with Data in it."

La Forge's artificial eyes widened. "What?"

"Commander Data was transferring hytritium from the trading vessel *Jovis* to the *Enterprise*-D via that shuttle. On the final transfer, the *Pike* was destroyed with Data inside—your sensor analysis revealed sufficient material to account for Data's remains in the explosion. You mourned his passing—until it was revealed that Data was alive, kidnapped by the *Jovis*'s shipmaster in an elaborate ruse."

"I know all that. I was *there.* But I'm not too clear on what this has to do with anything."

T'Lana regarded the chief engineer. Taking great care with her tone, she said, "I find that fascinating, Geordi, because I saw the connection as soon as I read Data's service record. For that matter, you yourself were reported killed in a transporter accident on stardate 45902, along with another officer. Data held a funeral service for you. On stardate 47135, Captain Picard was reported dead of a phaser blast on Dessica II, complete with eyewitness accounts and DNA evidence. In all three cases, the evidence of the person's death was as clear as it was with Data on the *Scimitar*—indeed, one might say more so."

Standing up suddenly, La Forge turned his back on T'Lana and stared out the port. "So you're saying that I . . . that I'm expecting Data to be alive? That's crazy."

"Is it? Leaving aside the three cases I mentioned, how often have members of this crew faced certain death and survived?"

La Forge sighed and started pacing across the office. "Look, I don't deny that we've been lucky more than once. But not everyone was. Tasha Yar died, and she stayed that way. Just a couple of weeks ago, Sara Nave and Lio Battaglia were killed by the Borg. I still have nightmares about Helga Van Mayter. She fell through a bulkhead that phased out of existence for half a second, then re-formed around her—it was one of the ugliest deaths I've ever seen. Counselor, I know precisely how permanent death is, and—"

T'Lana waited as the silence stretched out. Finally she asked, "And?"

"Nothing." La Forge sat back down. "Look, I realize you may see a connection, but it's not there. I'm *not* expecting Data to come back. I mean, yeah, every once in a while I walk onto the bridge, and I expect to see him sitting there at ops, or I'm waiting for him to come down to engineering, but we worked together for fifteen years! He is my best friend."

"And you don't wish to say good-bye to him—as evidenced by your once again using the present tense."

"He's still my friend. The fact that he's dead doesn't change that." La Forge shook his head. "Counselor, he . . . he was *Data*. He was stronger than any of us, smarter than any of us, gentler than any of us. He should've lived long enough to see the end of the universe." He lowered his hands and turned his electronic gaze upon T'Lana. "I don't know, maybe I don't want to say good-bye to her because that means admitting—"

"To *her*?"

"What?" La Forge cocked his head. "I didn't say 'to her'—did I?"

T'Lana nodded. "You did." She hesitated. "I do understand that one of the complaints made against those in my profession is that we tend to trace far too many neuroses to the patient's parents.

However, I believe there is a human saying about the shoe fitting."

That prompted a chuckle from La Forge. "Yeah. Damn. All these years, and it all goes back to Mom, doesn't it?"

"All too often, that is the case," T'Lana said.

"Is it with you?"

"No. I am Vulcan."

Smiling, La Forge said, "Vulcans don't have neuroses?"

"Vulcans do have neuroses far greater and more complex than those of many humanoids. We are not emotionless creatures. Quite the opposite—our emotions are far more turbulent than those of the surliest Klingon. We have learned to suppress them to our benefit, but that does not mean that there cannot be emotional trauma or difficulties." T'Lana leaned back. "However, my parents have always wholeheartedly supported my choices, including joining Starfleet."

"So did mine—but then they both are Starfleet."

T'Lana said nothing about this use of present tense. La Forge's mother, Captain Silva La Forge, was officially listed as missing and presumed dead. It had been so for nine years, since the disappearance of the *U.S.S. Hera.* La Forge's father was still alive and well. It seemed the commander did not deal well with death, or rather a death that he did not witness, where there was no body. Troi had noted this in her session notes. The Betazoid had tried drawing La Forge out but with little success. She had even admitted in her notes that perhaps

her friendship with La Forge could have handi-
capped the counseling sessions. T'Lana used what
she felt was her greatest asset. As a Vulcan, many
humans felt freer telling her their stories; it was not
logical, but it was true. By just listening she could
find what was troubling them.

"Tell me about them," T'Lana said.

The rest of La Forge's session consisted of the
chief engineer opening up to her, telling stories
about his parents, his sister. T'Lana noticed that La
Forge was open and honest with her. She believed
she could help him.

When the time was up, La Forge got to his feet.

"Thanks, Counselor. I guess I've got a lot to think
about."

"If you wish to speak again, Geordi, I would be
happy to schedule regular sessions."

Nodding, La Forge said, "Let me think about
that. One more thing."

"What is that?"

"Everyone calls me Geordi. But every time
Miranda does it, I flinch." He hesitated, seemed to
come to a decision, then said, "Maybe it's time I
told Miranda it's okay to call me Geordi too."

"You just said that she does already."

"Yeah, but I still want to give the permission."

"Then do so."

T'Lana had received the notice from Commander
Worf that Q had shown up and that all personnel

were under orders to ignore Q if he appeared. T'Lana found the tactic a sound one and assumed that Captain Picard had conceived it, based on his greater experience with Q.

Miranda Kadohata was here to discuss strategies to keep the crew calm, as Q had a tendency to provoke a response.

T'Lana began, "Commander, I believe that I . . ." She noticed that Kadohata was not listening. "Miranda, is there a problem?"

The second officer took a deep breath, "I feel like such a hypocrite. Here I am looking to enforce an order to ignore Q . . . when he popped into sickbay, it took everything I had to keep from belting him."

T'Lana's eyebrow shot up. "Such a gesture would have been—"

"Futile, I know, which is why I *didn't* do it. But I kept thinking about poor Ric." Before T'Lana could ask, Kadohata explained, "Ric Torres. He was a conn officer on the D back when it first launched. When Q showed up on the bridge, Ric pulled a phaser on him, and Q froze him solid. Sickbay managed to get him unfrozen, but Ric was never the same after that."

"You knew him?"

"We were lovers at the time—had been for a year previous. We came to the D together from the *Firenze,* and—" She looked down, as if embarrassed to be sharing her emotions with a Vulcan. "After what happened with Q, Ric wasn't the same. He broke it off with me, and eventually he transferred off, resigned his commission, started doing shuttle pilot work."

"And you blame Q?"

"Yes, I bloody well do! Ric was a right mess after that, and nothing I, or Counselor Troi, could do would set it right."

"Are you concerned about how this will affect you on the mission?"

"I'm concerned about me and the rest of the crew . . . Honestly, I haven't even *thought* about Ric in ten years. I just . . . I just don't know if I can trust myself to keep calm."

"Tell me," T'Lana said after a moment, "do you find yourself getting angry at your children?"

Snorting, Kadohata said, "I understand. I should act the way I do when Aoki does some typical five-year-old thing."

"Precisely."

T'Lana allowed herself a slight upturn of her mouth. "Q is very much like a small child. He can be petulant, moody—"

"—and bloody dangerous when he's careless and not paying attention."

"Which is why Captain Picard's suggestion of ignoring him is a good one—particularly for you."

Kadohata nodded. "You're right. Oh, and it was Worf's idea to ignore him."

"Indeed?"

T'Lana made a mental note to speak to the first officer. *I think,* she thought, *that it's past time we did so.* T'Lana had had issues with Worf's appointment as first officer, because he had put his personal desires before his duty during a critical mission. However, she was also willing to reconsider her hypothesis that Worf was unfit to command. The fact that it was he, rather than Picard, who suggested ignoring Q indicated a depth to the Klingon that deserved consideration.

"Counselor, one more thing. The crew seems off, on edge. I just wish there was something more I could do."

"This crew has been through a great deal of late. The wisest course of action, Miranda, would be to continue to do your duty."

Kadohata looked thoughtful. "I need to do more than my duty." Then she got a faraway look on her face. "Perhaps that's the ticket."

T'Lana asked, "Ticket?"

"Tradition. Tell me, T'Lana, have you ever played poker?"

10

———◆———

Karemma trading vessel *Shakikein*
Gamma Quadrant

One day before the end of the universe

VOGUSTA HATED SPACE TRAVEL.

He understood the need for it, of course. After all, one could not succeed in business if one remained on the Karemma homeworld. It was a useful base of operations, naturally—what better place to find a Karemma businessperson than on Karemma? But limiting oneself to that spot was just that: limiting. The Ferengi had a saying for it, as they seemed to for everything: "Home is where the heart is, but the stars are made of currency." Vogusta had always thought the saying to be lacking in clarity—the rib cage was where the heart was, and stars weren't actually made of currency at all—but he appreciated the greater meaning.

If only it didn't require actually *traveling* in space . . .

Intellectually, of course, Vogusta knew that the bulkhead wasn't going to crack or collapse or implode or explode or do any of the hundreds of other things it might do to expose Vogusta, Vogusta's cargo, Shipmaster Darsook, and Darsook's entire crew to the pitiless vacuum of space. Emotionally, though, he was expecting it to happen at any second.

When he had hired the *Shakikein* to take him to the Gaia system to meet with DaiMon Neek, a stipulation of the hire was that Vogusta's cabin was to be in the central part of the vessel, with no portals to the outside. He couldn't imagine any reason why he would be summoned to the flight deck, but if he was, all viewers were to show computer-generated sensor images rather than image translations of same. He wanted nothing to remind him that he was in the middle of an airless nothingness that would render him dead.

It was the only way he could get through the voyage.

As it was, he had to turn down two cheaper ships—a Dosi freighter and another Karemma vessel—because they could not meet those requirements. Still, even the *Shakikein*'s higher price was more cost-effective than trying to convince Neek to divert all the way to the Karemma homeworld.

Neek's ship, the *Windfall,* was going to the Vahni Vahtupali, which was half a dozen sectors in the other direction from the anomaly that led to this region of space—what those on the other side of the anomaly called "the Gamma Quadrant"—from Ferengi space. Diverting all the way to Karemma would have taken Neek too far out of his way for it to be worth the extra time.

So if Vogusta wanted his *kanar,* he had to travel to Gaia. He had several clients who had developed a taste for the Cardassian beverage during the period when the Cardassian Union—a military federation from the Ferengi side of the anomaly—had been absorbed by the Dominion. Although that period lasted only three years, many in the Gamma Quadrant desired the drink and were willing to pay two hundred *ilecs* for a case. (Vogusta himself couldn't stand the stuff, but who was he to get in the way of his clients' desires?) At that price, Vogusta could offer Neek a slip of gold-pressed latinum—or its equivalent in trade—per case and earn himself a tidy profit.

Neek was, of course, gouging Vogusta charging that much, but Vogusta didn't mind as long as he earned a profit. Were he a Ferengi, he would have paid Neek only half a slip a case and resold it for two hundred *ilecs* each, but the Karemma didn't do business in so distasteful a manner. Not that it mattered. Vogusta was able to make a good living; Vogusta's clients had all the *kanar* they could guzzle, and Neek made a tidy profit.

According to Shipmaster Darsook, the *Shakikein*

would be arriving at Gaia shortly. Vogusta was currently lying in his hammock, reading over the trade reports. He saw that Hanok had been elected to the position of chief overseer for the Commercial Authority for a second term, and that Clia and Ryno had successfully negotiated for the exclusive rights to distribute the music of the Anndii, whose *leolia* songs had become very popular.

"Vogusta, this is the flight deck. Please respond."

The words from the communications system startled Vogusta out of his hammock. He fell to the deck with a minimum of grace and a maximum of pain to his hip. Clambering to his feet, he wondered why in the name of the Founders the flight deck would need to speak to him.

Putting his hand to the intercom control, it activated. "This is Vogusta. To whom am I speaking?"

"Sir, this is Operator Zali. You have an external call from DaiMon Neek."

That surprised Vogusta—he didn't expect to speak to Neek until they arrived at Gaia tomorrow morning. "Put it through please, Operator."

"Yes, sir."

The screen on the wall shimmered to reveal the snaggletoothed smile of Neek. *"Greetings, Vogusta."*

"To you as well, DaiMon. To what do I owe this call?"

"Oh, you don't owe me anything—yet." Neek laughed at his own inferior joke. *"We've already arrived at Gaia—turns out our layover at Deep Space 9 was a bit shorter than anticipated."*

"I see. I could ask Shipmaster Darsook to increase speed, but we have been traveling at the vessel's maximum safe—"

Neek waved his hand in front of his face. *"No, no, don't bother. The Vahni said they'd be late for their rendezvous, so I don't profit by you arriving sooner. Besides, my engineer is using this as an excuse to find more things wrong with the* Windfall *that he can make me pay his brother's exorbitant repair prices for."*

Shaking his head, Vogusta said, "I do not understand your people's need to exploit."

"And I do not understand your people's lack of desire to. I'm amazed you've all stayed in business. In any case, I've got your three cases."

Vogusta frowned. "I ordered five."

"You were lucky to get the three. Prices went up again. Cardassia's economy isn't what it used to be. Kanar exports are one of the few things their government can actually make money on, so up the prices went. Don't even talk to me about the tariffs. I'm going to have to charge you one and a half slips per case."

Under normal circumstances, Vogusta would have haggled—a practice he abhorred but that the Ferengi insisted upon—but he had a better offer in any case. "I think what I have to trade will meet whatever price you name, DaiMon."

His beady little eyes widening, his round mouth falling open, Neek spoke in a whisper. *"You have the ink?"*

"Three boxes of it. Shall we say a box per case of *kanar*?"

Neek recovered. *"That's ridiculous. It's not worth that much."*

"It's worth more than that, Neek. You said you'd pay any price for the Leyles ink."

"I never said that."

Vogusta had expected that. "Shall I play you the recording of our conversation on the subject?"

"You recorded our conversations?" Neek asked, outraged.

"Of course. While the Karemma do not have anything as eloquent as your Rules of Acquisition, DaiMon, we do have certain codes of conduct that direct our actions. That code includes an instruction that has become nigh inviolable in the ten years since your people and ours first encountered each other: always record a conversation with a Ferengi."

"Recordings can be faked," Neek said sourly.

Vogusta shrugged. "If that is your attitude, DaiMon, then I will return to Karemma with my Leyles ink, and you can proceed to meet the Vahni." He moved to close the connection, knowing full well that he wouldn't get the chance.

Sure enough, Neek screamed, *"Wait!"*

"Yes?"

Neek stared angrily at Vogusta over the viewer. For more than a year, Neek had been asking after Leyles ink. The secretions of a very rare aquatic creature from the Leyles system contained an aphrodisiac and was sometimes used in tattoos. Using Leyles ink for body art created a state of permanent bliss. Vogusta thought it a barbaric practice, but Neek had insisted that he would "pay any price" to obtain the ink.

Neek couldn't afford to let Vogusta get away. The reason his profit margin was so high was that Neek didn't report the business he did in this quadrant, and he didn't pay taxes on it. Apparently Ferenginar had instituted a taxation system, a policy Neek violently disagreed with. While the Ferengi Commerce Authority had eyes all over the Ferengi side of the anomaly, they had many fewer on this side. Neek could do business "under the table," as he had phrased it.

Vogusta didn't care, as long as business got done. Neek had been a reliable client, and that was all that mattered.

Finally, Neek broke into a pointy-toothed grin. *"Sometimes I'm reminded why I like doing business with you, Vogusta. Your honesty is very refreshing."*

"If you say so," Vogusta said with a sigh. "So we have a deal?"

"Three boxes of Leyles ink for one of the cases of kanar."

The haggling again. "Three boxes for all three cases, DaiMon, or I take my business elsewhere. I'm sure if I have Shipmaster Darsook take us through the anomaly, I can find any number of sources of *kanar* at more reasonable prices *and* who'd be willing to take the ink off my ha—"

"Fine, fine," Neek said quickly, *"one box per case of* kanar." He smiled. *"I'll see you in the morning, Vogusta."*

The wall shimmered as Neek's face faded from view. Shaking his head, Vogusta returned to his hammock and continued reading until he fell asleep.

He was awakened by the voice of Operator Zali again saying, *"Vogusta, this is the flight deck. Please respond."*

Blinking himself awake—Vogusta had always been a light sleeper—he got out of the hammock. Noting the time on the display unit, he realized that they were probably arriving at Gaia. He placed his hand on the intercom control. "This is Vogusta."

"Sir, Shipmaster Darsook has requested your presence on the flight deck."

"What for?" Vogusta asked, trying to keep the revulsion out of his voice. Darsook's people were going to handle the transfer with the Ferengi. They didn't need him walking around the ship, and especially not on the flight deck, which was only one small thin bulkhead away from space.

"We've arrived at the coordinates, sir, and Shipmaster Darsook feels you should be present for this."

Testily, Vogusta said, "Operator, please inform Shipmaster Darsook that I'm familiar with what the Gaia system looks like, as well as the general design of the *Windfall,* and that I fail to see what's to be gained by having me—"

"Vogusta, this is Darsook."

That brought Vogusta up short. Darsook rarely used the communications system himself, preferring to have his lackeys handle it. "Shipmaster, what's—"

"We've arrived at the coordinates, but there is no sign of Gaia—or of the Windfall.*"*

"That's not possible. I just spoke with DaiMon Neek last night."

"I know, and that was my first reaction when Operator Veste informed me, but the sensor readings are quite definitive—at least in telling us what isn't *there."*

"I don't understand."

Did Vogusta hear the shipmaster sigh? *"Which is why I have requested your presence on the flight deck. It would be far easier to explain if you could see it."*

Vogusta didn't like to see space. It was full of icy comets, hot suns, airless asteroids and all sorts of awful radiation and, worst of all, no air to breathe. Aside from its necessity as the medium through which he had to travel to do business, Vogusta had no use for space and no need to see it.

But it was obvious that Darsook wasn't going to take "I don't want to" for an answer. Something strange was going on here, and if the *Windfall* was indeed missing, Vogusta had a big problem on his hands.

Reluctantly, he said, "I'll be right there."

As he navigated the narrow corridors of the *Shakikein,* Vogusta tried to keep his eyes shut as much as possible. This caused him to bump into a wall that curved to the left as he strode, scaring him out of his wits and sending him into convulsions and hyperventilation. Somehow, he got his breathing under control and arrived at the door to the tube.

Having memorized the tube system, and knowing how sturdy the shafts were, Vogusta felt safer here. But he was shaking so much his knees collided with each other as he walked out onto the flight deck.

His eyes first went to the viewscreen, even though he knew, just *knew* that it would be showing an exterior visual of space. Vogusta was about to complain about the fact that it showed an image translation, violating his contract. Then he saw the image.

He had no idea what it was. It appeared to be some kind of roiling mass of energy. There was nothing to indicate its size, as there was nothing else in view to compare it to. "What is that?"

"Glad you could join us, Vogusta," Darsook said wryly. "To answer your question—we have no idea."

"How . . . how big is it?"

Darsook looked forward and to his left at one of his crew. "Operator Danee, report to Vogusta."

One of the many Karemma who were staffing the stations that lined the sides of the flight deck turned around. "The distance between the event horizon and what we believe to be the epicenter of the phenomenon is greater than the distance between Gaia's sun and its outermost planet."

Horror filled Vogusta as he stared at the viewscreen. "It's swallowed the entire system?"

"We believe so, yes," Danee said.

Wrenching his gaze away from the horror on the viewer, he turned and asked the operator, "Any sign of the *Windfall*?"

"I'm afraid not, sir."

Vogusta couldn't believe it. "How could this have happened?"

"We don't know," Darsook said. "However, I have no intention of keeping my ship in this area. For all we know, this . . . this thing will expand."

Whirling to look back at the shipmaster, Vogusta asked, "Is there any evidence to support that?"

"No—and that's the problem. We don't have any evidence that this phenomenon even *exists,* except for our eyes. Our sensors do not detect it." His nostrils flared. "Vogusta, unless you give me a very good reason to remain, we are leaving Gaia immediately and returning to Karemma."

Vogusta said nothing, instead turning back to stare at the screen, wondering what happened to Neek and his crew, not to mention whoever might have lived in Gaia—at least one of its planets was inhabited.

"Vogusta?" Darsook prompted.

Shaking his head, Vogusta turned back to look at Darsook. "Yes, of course, Shipmaster, we must depart immediately." Moving toward the tube, he said quietly, "If you'll excuse me, I will return to my cabin now." He wanted to get as far away from the flight deck as he could.

11

———◆———

Enterprise
In orbit of Gorsach IX

One day before the end of the universe

"ALL RIGHT," GEORDI LA FORGE SAID AS HE STARED across the console at Ensign Taurik and Kadohata, "we need to get creative."

Taurik raised an eyebrow. "I fail to see what use creativity will be in this circumstance."

La Forge chuckled. Taurik was a good straight man. *Just like Data. Damn, where did that come from?*

"We've scanned every millimeter of the surface. We've found no signs of those animals you encountered."

"Q was right, by the by, about their being *yrilijk.* Whatever came after us looked just like the cave drawings on Berengaria." Kadohata let out a breath. "Honestly, if my tricorder hadn't made a record of the bloody things, I'd be convinced it was a hallucination."

"It is unlikely," Taurik said, "that the same hallucination was shared by Commander Worf, Lieutenant Leybenzon, and you."

Shaking his head, La Forge said, "Q's involved, Taurik. That means *all* bets are off."

"We could run an icogram," Kadohata said.

"That is an illogical request," Taurik said flatly. "An icospectrogram is generally run to determine the presence of dilithium. However, we already *know* there are dilithium deposits on the planet."

"I gotta agree with Taurik," La Forge said. "The icogram isn't gonna tell us anything we don't already know."

"That is precisely why I want to do the scan," she said.

Frowning, La Forge said, "I don't follow you."

"I was thinking back on some of the other examples I came across in the records of 'constructed' planets like this—in particular I was thinking about Talos IV. The Talosians were able to fool not only the *Enterprise* crew but also their sensors into thinking that the planet wasn't a nuclear wasteland. What if something—Q, or what have you—is doing the same thing here?"

"If that is the case," Taurik said, "then an icospectrogram would confirm the presence of dilithium."

"Or deny it. Discrepant data can be as useful as corroborating data, particularly when there's a wild card like Q and a planet that simply *cannot* exist."

"Of course it can!" said an all-too-familiar smarmy voice from behind La Forge. "There are more things in Heaven and Earth than are dreamt of in your philosophy. Jean-Luc's silly old Bard said that, and for once, he got it right."

Ignore him, La Forge told himself forcefully. He could see Kadohata tensing. However, Taurik was proceeding as if Q hadn't spoken. "Logical, I shall proceed."

"This whole thing is a waste of *time!*" Q said, materializing on the other side of the console from La Forge. "Why are you just standing around up here throwing all this technobabble around? Why not just go *down* there?"

Taurik said, "We should . . ."

Q rolled his eyes. "Here it comes. It amazes me that Vulcans even *managed* space travel, given how much time they've wasted on being pedantic." He grinned. "Of course, they developed space travel before they became boring, which probably explains it. Ah, the good ol' days before Surak—that's when your people *really* knew how to party."

Given Vulcan's history of brutal warfare before Surak united the planet with his tenets of logic, La Forge doubted "party" was the right word. But then, Q was just trying to get a response—or talking to hear himself talk.

Taurik, to his credit, didn't miss a beat. ". . . attempt a subspace differential scan."

Kadohata winced. "That might cause damage to the planet."

"I'm surrounded by imbeciles," Q said. "Why not just fire a few photon torpedoes at it?"

"If the planet is a construct," Taurik said, "then perhaps if we damage it, it will draw the attention of those who built it."

"I'm with Miranda," La Forge said. "That's way too risky right now. We could try a tachyon pulse, see if it detects any kind of cloak."

"Done," Kadohata said. "Worf suggested it. Didn't turn up a damn thing."

"This is pathetic." Q started pacing. "You're taking suggestions from *microbrain*? I never realized how much you people depended on Data. It's becoming blindingly obvious to me that he was carrying the lot of you."

La Forge continued to ignore Q. "What about the force field you guys came across? Any sign of where that came from?"

"No sign," Kadohata said, "and there's no EM energy down there whatsoever. We even did a psilosynine scan. It confirmed the medical scans. If whatever's down there is telepathic, it isn't of a kind we're familiar with."

Q said, "Oh, I just can't *stand* this anymore." He snapped his fingers and disappeared.

As soon as he did, La Forge smiled. "Y'know, I think that's the fastest we ever got rid of him."

"Wasn't fast enough, if you ask me," Kadohata muttered.

"I have the results of the icospectrogram, sir." Taurik handed Kadohata the padd.

Which wouldn't have been a problem, except La Forge also reached for it. At first, La Forge instinctively started to point out that Taurik worked for *him,* not her, but strictly speaking, that wasn't true. She was second officer. Aside from Worf and the captain, everyone on the ship worked for her.

"I'm sorry," La Forge said weakly.

"You're dismissed, Ensign." Commander Kadohata then turned and faced La Forge. He was amazed. If a subordinate officer had done that to him, he would not have been so calm.

"It's all right."

It didn't sound all right, based on the tone in Kadohata's voice, but La Forge figured he'd take it.

"The icogram shows exactly what we picked up on the surface." She handed him the padd. Kadohata added, "Look, Geordi, it really is all right. It always takes time to adjust to a new person in the double-play combination."

"The what?" La Forge asked with a frown.

"It's a baseball reference. The fielders who play the positions of second base and shortstop are generally referred to as the 'double-play combination,' as those two positions are the key component in the so-called double-play . . ." Miranda stopped herself. "But that's neither here nor there—we just need to adjust to each other, yeah?"

Smiling, La Forge said, "Yeah. And we can start with Gorsach IX."

"Well, I'm at a loss, to be honest. We've tried every scan, we've combined scans, we've done so many I've lost track of what we've done. We've so overcomplicated thi—" She cut herself off.

After Kadohata stood silent for a full five seconds, La Forge finally asked, "Uh, Miranda? You okay?"

She turned to La Forge. "You're going to think I've gone barmy."

"Miranda, we just found a perfect planet with a force field we can't detect. Extinct Berengarian animals that we also can't detect are keeping us out of one of the perfectly symmetrical caverns in the circular canyon, and we have Q showing up. We passed 'barmy' a while ago."

Kadohata took a breath. "There are three scans we've not yet attempted."

"There's no standard scan that we haven't performed," La Forge pointed out. "Hell, we've even done several nonstandard ones."

"Oh, these are *quite* nonstandard, Geordi. We're going to hit Gorsach IX with radio waves, magnetic resonance imaging, and X-rays."

La Forge couldn't help it. He laughed. It was the equivalent of asking Doctor Crusher to operate with catgut and scalpels, Leybenzon to use chemical explosives.

"Well, it's no crazier than the icogram. And the worst thing that'll happen is we improperly calibrate the emitters, the X-rays give us all radiation poisoning, and we die."

Kadohata grinned. "That's all?"

Chuckling, La Forge said, "Let's get to work."

Jean-Luc Picard picked up the wineglass and started twirling it, watching as the red wine sloshed up the sides of the crystal, the residue trailing down in straight lines. *Good legs,* he thought, then brought the glass to his nose. He got a whiff of berry with a bit of spice thrown in. The nose wasn't especially strong, but there was a variety there, at least. *And all things considered, that's better than could be expected.*

Across the table, Beverly Crusher was examining the label of the bottle. They had finished their dinner, their plates containing only the remnants of the filet mignon and the *sknort* casserole they'd shared. After they'd eaten, Picard poured the wine that he had decanted, on a whim, before dinner. It was a reserve vintage, 70 percent cabernet sauvignon, 20 percent cabernet franc, and 10 percent merlot, and was one of the *spécialités de la maison* of Château Picard.

"The label says twenty-three seventy-two. Isn't that—" Beverly hesitated.

Picard nodded, not quite ready to drink it yet. "Yes, this is the first batch after Robert and René died." The deaths of his brother and nephew in a fire had hit Picard hard when it happened nine years earlier. "It was difficult to deal with at first—I never really *liked* Robert, but I did love him. When I went home after . . . the Borg incident, we were finally able to bury the past. And René . . ." He trailed off. "A young life filled with promise . . ."

Looking up at Crusher, he said, "Their deaths made me realize how important it is to cherish what you have, to not assume it will always be there. I admit—in one particular case—it took some time for that lesson to sink in."

Beverly smiled at him. "Thick head or slow learner?"

Picard smiled. "A little of both. I suppose I should taste this." The captain sipped the wine and tried to hide his disappointment. "It would seem that Marie learned quite a bit over the past few years. The later vintage we drank in Data's honor was much . . . smoother."

"Has she taken over the winery?"

Setting the glass down, Picard said, "Marie always ran the vineyard herself. Robert knew the grapes better than anyone, but he had no head for business."

Smiling, Crusher said, "But her knowledge of wine came from Robert by osmosis?"

"Which is not the best teacher," Picard said with a nod. "She tried to hire the best vintners, but it was difficult to find anyone as good as Robert who wasn't already committed to another winery."

"Well, I'm glad she's gotten better." Crusher

reached out her hand to him. And Picard happily kissed it.

"Such domestic bliss. Such tranquillity. Such heartfelt joy. It's enough to make you throw up."

Picard whirled around to see Q standing in the doorway to the bedroom, wearing a monk's robe. He then recalled his own orders and turned back to Crusher.

"It's a waste of time, you know," Q said. "Trust me, as an old married man, this is a huge mistake. I mean, look at me and Q—we were companions for years, on and off, but once it came to a serious commitment, to reproducing, the whole thing went to pieces. First she couldn't get enough of little q, but then when he grew up, she couldn't handle it, and suddenly we weren't a couple anymore. Oh, sure, now she's back, but trust me, your best bet is to take a vow of celibacy."

"So," Picard said without paying any attention to Q, "how are the physicals coming?"

"Quite well, actually, though Lieutenant Leybenzon *still* hasn't reported in, even though Worf promised he'd talk to him."

Q shook his head. "I don't believe this. First La Forge and that dippy new second officer of yours, now you two. I'm being given the silent treatment? I knew the human race was infantile, Jean-Luc, but this is beyond the pale."

Picard offered, "I could remind him of his duty if you wish."

"I'd rather you didn't get into it yet, Jean-Luc,"

she said. "Besides, there are enough issues with us having a relationship—"

Q, along with a chair, materialized between the two of them at the table. Q was now wearing the captain's uniform he generally favored. "Which is one of about a thousand reasons why this is a stupid idea." He grinned. "Besides, do you really think the two of you can match the thrills of your past relationships?" Q snapped his fingers, and he transformed in a flash of light into Odan, the Trill diplomat with whom Crusher had fallen in love. "Will you recapture the joy of Odan?" he continued, still using Q's smarmy voice, which was something of a mixed blessing, as far as Picard was concerned. Another finger snap and he became Keith Hughes. "At least Doctor Hughes had something in common with you." The fingers of Hughes snapped, and in a flash of light he became Ronin, the creature who had made Crusher into his love slave on Caldos. "Can Jean-Luc match the sheer unbridled passion of Ronin?" In Q's voice, Ronin sniggered. "I doubt it."

Summoning all the willpower he had to bear, Picard stared at Crusher. "Do as you see fit, Beverly."

Q-as-Ronin snapped his fingers and became Vash, a woman Picard met on Risa. "As for you, Jean-Luc, do you *truly* think this drip of a doctor will give you Vash's lust for life?" Another finger snap, and he became Anij, the Ba'ku woman. "Or Anij's wisdom?" Then he became the youthful Marta Batanides, his old Academy friend, with whom he had never had any kind of romantic relationship. "And let's face it, we never get over our first love."

"Thank you, Jean-Luc," Crusher said, and Picard could hear the tension in her voice, "but I'm sure it'll all work out."

With an exasperated sigh, Q changed back to his own form, again in the Starfleet captain's uniform. "You people are just no fun at all."

And then he disappeared.

Crusher let out a long breath, and Picard could see the tension leaving her shoulders. "That was impossible. I so wanted to punch him—especially when he became Ronin." She looked at him. "Who was that last one he turned into?"

"It's a long story," Picard said quickly.

"Really?"

Sighing, Picard said, "Marta was one of my Academy classmates."

"I don't remember you ever telling me about her."

He deliberately left out the last name so Crusher wouldn't connect it with the high-ranking admiral in Starfleet Intelligence. "I'd really rather not discuss it, Beverly—it will simply start a protracted discussion about Q, which I'd just as soon avoid."

After giving him a look that made it clear that she was most assuredly *not* giving up this easily, but merely tabling the discussion for now, she said, "I wonder what Q wants."

Picking up the wineglass, Picard said, "I'm quite sure that Q will let us know in due course. He always does."

12

Malon *Supertanker Keta*
Delta Quadrant

One day before the end of the universe

"WE HAVE A PROBLEM—SHIELD NUMBER 2 IS FAILING."

Controller Sheel looked up sharply at Liswan's report. "What do you mean, shield number 2 is failing?"

Liswan frowned. "Which part of the sentence didn't you comprehend?"

Running a hand through his thinning brown-gold hair—and pulling out a few tufts, to his annoyance—Sheel said, "All of it—or, rather, none of it. What I don't comprehend is *why*."

"Remlap doesn't have that answer, sir. All she will say is that the shield is failing."

"Why am I not surprised? Tell her to *fix* it."

Shaking her head, Liswan said, "She can't."

"Why not?"

"Because she doesn't know the cause," Liswan said slowly, as if speaking to a child. Sheel had to resist the urge to punch her in her gold-skinned nose. "Can't really fix it unless—"

"Fine, fine. How soon until it fails?"

"She isn't sure—"

"—how long that will be, either, of course." Sheel peered down at his console, located in the center of the tanker's bridge.

"But the most we have is twelve hours," Liswan said. "The problem is, when the shield fails, we'll all be exposed to the theta radia—"

Angrily turning on his first mate, Sheel said, "Are you laboring under the delusion that I don't know what'll happen when the shield fails?"

"Well," Liswan said with a shrug, "you didn't know what 'Shield number 2 is failing' meant, so I thought it'd be better to be safe than—"

"Liswan, be *quiet,*" Sheel snapped, then turned back to the console. They were on course for system KMH-5, which had an O-type star where they could dump their antimatter waste. In order to achieve faster-than-light travel, the Malon used a matter/antimatter annihilation drive, which created a waste product that was teeming with theta radiation. Other worlds had learned the trick of eliminating the waste, but the Malon had not. In his more cynical moods, the controller thought that the government kept it that way, because waste disposal was a major source of revenue. Without the need for supertankers like the *Keta*, shipyards would lose major contracts, and the people building them would be unemployed. The Malon had enough economic hardships these days, especially since the Vidiian Sodality levied trade sanctions (ever since they were cured of that disease, they'd been putting on airs), the Haakonians stopped buying Malon *therhea* grain, and the *smap* crop had gone bad for the third year in a row.

However, dumping the waste was getting more and more difficult, as they were running out of places to dump it. A controller named Emck had done good business dumping the waste in a place called the "Void," but a strange vessel from a faraway sector—the so-called ship of death—had stopped him. That left contracts open to other contractors who could find places to get the waste disposed.

The hard part was finding a place to dump the waste that was close enough to reach before the ships' shields failed. Sheel had found an O-type star, but it was four months from the Malon homeworld at the maximum safe cruising speed. They were only one day out at the moment, but if the shield failed . . .

Only one thing to do. He turned to Refeek at the flight control console against the bridge's starboard bulkhead. "Increase to maximum."

Refeek whirled around and squinted at him. "Controller, we're *at* maximum."

Glowering at the young man, Sheel said, "No, we're at our maximum safe *cruising* speed. I want us to go to our *emergency* speed."

"Sir," Refeek said, casting a furtive glance at Liswan, "regulations say that we can go to emergency speed only in . . . well, an emergency."

Looking down, as if hoping the deck would provide comfort—it didn't—Sheel let out a long breath. He had hired Refeek only because he was willing to work more cheaply, a cost-cutting measure whose efficacy the controller was now questioning. "Refeek, one of our shields is about to collapse."

"Well, we have three of them, don't we?" Refeek asked. "I mean, don't we have three so that if one fails the other two will keep it going?"

Swearing never again to skimp on pilot salaries, assuming he lived that long, Sheel said, "No, we have three because we don't have enough power on this ship to run four." Sheel had heard that a tanker called the *Apsac* had managed the trick of getting seven shields running simultaneously, but Sheel had never seen any proof of that, and besides, the *Apsac* disappeared four years ago without a trace. "Besides," he went on, "do you know how many instances of shield failure there have been where the other shields didn't immediately collapse in a cascade effect?"

His voice very small now, Refeek said, "Er, no. Three, maybe?"

"It's a trick question, Refeek—the answer is none. As soon as that shield goes down, it'll be a matter of seconds before the others go with it. In fact, it could happen at any second, and I'd hate to think that we all died of theta radiation poisoning because of the precious time we lost because you were asking *stupid questions*!"

Throughout, Sheel's voice had been rising in volume, to the point where Refeek actually flinched at the last two words. He increased the ship's speed.

"Uh, sir," Liswan said quickly, "that may not be such a good idea. The shields may not be able to tolerate—"

"Liswan, is there any chance that we'll make it to KMH-5 at our current speed before the shield collapses?"

"Well, no," Liswan said. "Remlap said it'd be—"

"—twelve hours at the most. If we increase speed, there's a chance we'll make it to KMH-5 before the shield collapses. If we *don't* increase speed, there's *no* chance we'll make it. I don't know about you, but I know which option I prefer."

Nodding, Liswan said, "I withdraw my objection, Controller."

Dryly, Sheel said, "Very generous of you. Now if you'd be so kind as to go down to Remlap and see if—"

Controller Sheel did not finish his sentence. A strange anomaly suddenly appeared in the space that the *Keta* was occupying. Had Sheel not ordered the increase in speed, the *Keta* might have detected the anomaly before colliding with it—but it might not have, since Malon supertankers do not come equipped with viewscreens. The Malons never developed that technology, having never had the need to provide themselves with image translations of sensor data. Malons generally preferred the readings provided to them by their computers and scanning equipment. Indeed, when the first Malon set foot on a vessel of alien design, she had been surprised to see that they had viewscreens and believed it to be an extravagance.

For that reason, Sheel and his crew might never have noticed the anomaly, since their sensors would not have been able to detect it. Instead it, and the two million isotons of antimatter waste it was carrying inside of tanks that were inadequately protected by three shields, one of which was in danger of collapse, simply disappeared.

13

—◆—

Enterprise
In orbit of Gorsach IX

The day the universe ends

WORF CHANGED OUT OF HIS *MOK'BARA* UNIFORM in his quarters and allowed himself a smile.

I am happy.

They were three words he rarely had cause to use in succession. His four years as the Federation ambassador to the Klingon Empire were productive ones, allowing him to serve both his homeworld and his adopted home. Worf had surprised himself by becoming a good diplomat, but it was not a career that fulfilled his needs.

A new Federation president had been elected,

and as was expected Worf offered his letter of resignation. While he was being pressed on all sides to stay, Worf realized that he had his fill of diplomacy and politics. No sooner had Worf regained his commission than he was once again assigned to the *Enterprise*. That was the last time, Worf recalled. The last time he remembered thinking he was happy.

This was the life he was meant to lead.

The morning *Mok'bara* class had been well attended—Leybenzon had brought Stolovitzky and de Lange, and Doctor Tropp was progressing to where he no longer was a danger to other students.

"Commander," said a pleasant voice from behind him as Worf left his quarters, "I was just coming to see you."

Turning around, Worf saw the small, graceful form of T'Lana. "Counselor," he said. "I am on my way to the bridge. You may accompany me."

"Thank you."

She fell into step with Worf as they approached the turbolift. To his surprise, she was able to keep pace with him. Worf was silently appreciative. He still did not know what to make of T'Lana. She had opposed Worf's appointment to the position of first officer and had disagreed with the captain throughout the encounter with the Borg. While they seemed to come to some kind of rapprochement after the incident, Worf felt that T'Lana was not comfortable with him in a command position.

After a few seconds, T'Lana spoke. "Your suggestion of ignoring Q was an excellent one, Commander. The tactic is psychologically sound—as far as one might determine the psychology of a being such as Q."

Worf looked down at her as they walked. "His personality has proved remarkably consistent every time he has appeared." As they approached the turbolift, Worf touched the call control.

"I've never encountered him, of course," T'Lana said, "but I have read about Q in Starfleet reports. I find his apparent fascination with the Federation in general and humanity in particular to be intriguing."

"That is not the adjective I would have used," Worf said in a dry tone.

"Understandably, since your concerns during your other encounters were related to the security of the ship. But I find his obsession to be quite odd for one of his powers and capabilities."

The lift arrived, and they entered. "Bridge," Worf said, then he added to T'Lana, "Q would have us believe that we are beyond his understanding."

Before T'Lana could respond, Worf found himself briefly blinded by a flash of light. When it cleared, Q stood between them, wearing one of his smugger smiles.

"Absolutely, you're beyond my understanding. The sooner you figure *that* out, microbrain, the happier you'll be."

Worf found it remarkably easy to follow his own orders. He'd spent the last four years listening to the incessant prattle that was part and parcel of a diplomat's life. After that, ignoring Q was quite simple.

"And as for *you*," Q said to T'Lana, "stop trying to drown me in your tiresome psychobabble. I'm a Q. We don't *have* psychologies or neuroses or any of those other tiresome personality issues that you mortals have. We've evolved beyond such things."

Now Worf was interested. He wondered if T'Lana's Vulcan curiosity about Q's psychology might lead her to respond to Q's comment, giving him the attention he craved.

T'Lana merely looked straight ahead and said nothing.

Worf stood ramrod straight in the turbolift, also saying nothing.

Q let out a long sigh. "What was I thinking? I wasn't going to get any love from the Geordi-and-Randy show, and Jean-Luc and Beverly are as tiresome as ever. I must have been mad to think I could get a rise out of a Vulcan and the galaxy's glummest Klingon."

With another flash of light, he was gone.

"A pity," T'Lana said. "I would have liked the opportunity to question him."

"It is well that you did not," Worf said.

"Of course. Your orders were, as I said, quite correct."

The doors parted on the bridge. Picard was just getting up from the command chair.

Picard said, "Excellent, Number One, Counselor, I was about to summon you. Commanders Kadohata and La Forge believe they have found something on the surface." The captain moved toward the observation lounge. "Mister Leybenzon, join us."

La Forge, Crusher, and Kadohata were already present when Worf took his seat beside Picard. Kadohata was holding a padd, pacing beside the observation ports.

"Commander," Picard said, "you have information."

Kadohata nodded. "Yes, but you'll never believe how we got it, sir."

"All day," La Forge put in, "we tried every scan we knew, but nothing revealed the source of the force field Lieutenant Leybenzon hit, or the *yrilijk* that defended the cavern. So Miranda decided to try something a little less sophisticated."

Smiling, Kadohata said, "We bombarded the beamdown site with X-rays, magnetic resonance imaging, and radio waves."

"You're kidding." Crusher sounded appalled.

Holding up his hands, La Forge said, "I know it sounds crazy, but we'd tried everything else."

"And you found?"

"The X-ray and MRI gave us something rather interesting." Kadohata activated the holoviewer.

The upper-left-hand corner lit up with an ordinary visual image of one of the caverns in the canyon. Kadohata said, "This is the cavern in question." She touched another control, and the upper-right-hand corner lit up with a schematic of the cavern, interior and exterior, with callouts indicating molecular composition, chemical analysis, and more. "Here's what sensors gave us, including about a dozen different specific scans. All of it's about what you'd expect." The cavern matched Worf's memory, a twisting corridor of rock, lasting about thirty meters before dead-ending.

Giving a half smile, Kadohata touched another control. "Now here's the fun bit." Two images filled in the bottom half. The one on the left, under the visual image, was displayed in several bright colors, which varied according to the density of the object in question. The one on the right showed only black and white and gray.

Worf sat up straight as he realized what he was seeing. The cavern entrance and the first ten meters matched on all four images, but once you went past that point, the MRI and X-ray images showed not a curving continuation of the cavern into a cul-de-sac but rather a widening corridor of rock that angled downward, finally opening into a huge area several meters wide.

Leybenzon was leaning so far forward in his chair that Worf half expected him to fall out of it. "The topography does not match."

"Got it in one, Lieutenant," Kadohata said. "There's something in that cavern that some*one* doesn't want us to see."

"And we were lucky to find this at all," La Forge added.

Worf turned to Picard. "Captain, we *must* send another away team and a well-armed security force to penetrate the force field."

Leybenzon said, "I can have a team prepared immediately, sir."

"I don't think that's such a hot idea, sir," La Forge said.

"Nor I." Kadohata sat down between La Forge and Crusher as she spoke. "We know what we do only because it never occurred to whoever built this to shield against primitive scanning techniques."

"You're saying we got lucky," Crusher said.

"More than that." La Forge shook his head. "We saw what we saw because we're stupider than they expected us to be. That doesn't bode well for our odds."

Worf understood the chief engineer's caution but did not share it. "Perhaps they simply were hoping that no one would examine their deception too carefully. That indicates an enemy who might grow careless. We should take advantage of that."

The captain took in everyone's comments. He had a look on his face that Worf had come to know well over the years he served under Picard, and he had also seen it on the faces of Sisko and Martok: a commanding officer weighing everything, adding in countless other factors that few in the room even knew about, before coming to a decision.

"Bridge to Captain."

Looking up, Picard said, "Go ahead, Lieutenant."

"Sir, you have a priority-one communiqué from Admiral Janeway at Starfleet Command."

Now Worf saw a different expression on his captain's face, and it wasn't a pleasant one. Picard had disobeyed Janeway's direct orders when they engaged the Borg. Worf had suspected the reason the *Enterprise* was assigned to explore the remote Gorsach system was to get the ship and her captain out of Janeway's hair.

With only the slightest hint of regret in his voice—Worf doubted that Leybenzon, Kadohata, and T'Lana detected it—the captain said, "Pipe it in here, Lieutenant."

The four images of the cavern on Gorsach IX were replaced by the familiar face of Kathryn Janeway—which looked, as Worf expected, grim—sitting in her office at Starfleet Headquarters.

"Admiral Janeway," Picard said. "What can we do for you?"

Janeway said, *"This isn't a social call, as you might imagine, Captain. We've been receiving reports over the past day or so of spatial rifts opening all over the galaxy."*

Frowning, Picard said, "What kind of rifts?"

"That's just it," Janeway said, *"we don't know. They're not showing up on any kind of sensor scan. We do know that they're all spherical but varying in diameter. Some of them have swallowed up entire star systems, while others are no larger than an asteroid. But several dozen ships have gone missing, and these rifts may have claimed billions of lives already. No kind of scan is picking them up—we can see them, but that's it.*

"It's not just the Alpha Quadrant, either," the admiral continued. "Titan, Ganymede, *and the*

Klingons have reported rifts in the Beta Quadrant, Deep Space 9 has reported several instances that have been relayed to them from the Gamma Quadrant, and Project Voyager has been keeping in touch with several allies we made in the Delta Quadrant who've been reporting the same."

"We have seen no such rifts here, Admiral," Picard said.

"We've mapped the rifts' appearances, and they're occurring in a very specific pattern. The epicenter of that pattern is the Gorsach system."

Picard sat up. Worf stiffened.

Before either could comment, however, the sound of slow clapping came from the other end of the table. Turning, Worf saw that Q had appeared at the far end of the table, facing Picard, now wearing an admiral's uniform.

"Bravissimo! You've finally figured it out. I did warn you that this was a pivotal place in the universe."

"Q, what kind of game are you playing?" That was Janeway. Worf recalled that Janeway's former command, *Voyager,* had encountered Q on several occasions, and that Q's offspring considered Janeway to be his godmother. Based on the look on the admiral's face, it was an honor she would have preferred to decline.

"Ah, Kathy, always a pleasure to lay eyes on your lovely visage."

"The pleasure is all yours," Janeway said tightly.

Q snickered. "The admiral's bars suit you, you

know—now you have a whole *fleet* to annoy, instead of just a few random nincompoops on that garden spade with a pituitary problem you commanded." Q then turned to Picard. "Well, then, Jean-Luc, have you seen enough?"

Abandoning the ploy of ignoring Q, Picard asked, "Seen enough of what?"

Shaking his head, Q said, "My my my my, you *have* gone dense. Gorsach IX. You just walked into a cavern and wiped out billions of lives."

"Are you saying that our intrusion *caused* these rifts to open?"

"Yup, completely dense." Q rolled his eyes. "Wake up, Jean-Luc—those rifts opened the very *microsecond* your trained monkey over there"—he pointed at Leybenzon—"went into the cavern."

Turning to the viewer, Picard asked, "Admiral, is that true?"

Janeway looked nonplussed. *"As far as we can tell, the rifts all popped up at about the same time."*

Worf asked, "When?"

"Twenty-three hours ago."

"Bloody hell," Kadohata muttered. "Captain, ship's time is about zero-eight hundred, and it was at zero-nine hundred yesterday that we entered that last cavern."

"What is it with you people," Q asked, "that you have to take half an hour to figure out what I already told you?"

Kadohata almost sneered at Q. "Probably something to do with not trusting you."

"Yes, well, Randy dear, I'm afraid that trust isn't the issue here—survival is."

Next to him, Worf saw Leybenzon start to rise. Putting a hand on the security chief's shoulder, Worf shook his head.

Without even looking at Worf or Leybenzon, Q said, "Oh, you should let him try it, microbrain. I've been waiting for an excuse to turn this one into a newt."

"Q, enough of this," Janeway said. *"Give us a straight answer for once in your misbegotten life."*

Grinning, Q said, "Oh, Kathy, why start now?" He let out a breath. "But seriously, folks, do you really need little ol' me to spell it out for you?"

"Humor us, Q," Picard said. Worf noted that the captain's hands were clasped tightly in front of him.

"Oh, very well, since you've apparently all taken your stupid pills this morning. That planet down there is *dangerous.* Just by setting foot in the wrong spot, you've started a universewide catastrophe."

Noting Q's choice of words, Worf said, "Universe? These rifts extend beyond this galaxy?"

"Give that Klingon a cigar!" Q snapped his fingers, and a lit cigar appeared in the first officer's mouth. Worf had first encountered the vile leaves wrapped in paper as a boy on Gault, when Uncle Yuri had given him one, and he had no wish to relive the experience. Yanking the cigar out of his mouth, he stubbed it out on his hand and glared at Q, who, naturally, was still talking: "Your brain is actually becoming less micro by the second—yes, these phenomena are occurring all over the universe, claiming far more than the billions of lives dear Kathy was concerned about. That's what happened when you stood on the threshold. Going in would be insanely suicidal and stupid, and if I were you, I'd get the hell out of the system—or at least out of orbit. Those two gas giants look like they might be fun to look at. I can assure you that they're free of anything that might spell certain death for the universe as we know it."

Standing up, Picard announced the decision he had just made. "That settles it, then. I'm going down there."

Q's face fell. "Jean-Luc, you can't be serious."

Picard walked over to the other end of the table and shoved his face into Q's. "If you're *that* insistent that we not beam down to the planet, then I feel the best course of action we can take is to beam down posthaste."

Q said, "Kathy, you outrank him, and you've proved yourself to have at least a modicum of sense. Order him not to."

It was with a profound sense of relief that Worf heard the words, *"Captain Picard, you have my full support in your exploration of the surface of Gorsach IX. I only ask that you report your findings with dispatch."*

Picard looked at Janeway and smiled. "Thank you, Admiral."

"Starfleet out." Janeway's image faded from the viewer.

Q disappeared in a flash of light and reappeared between Picard and Worf.

"Jean-Luc, listen to me," Q said insistently, "the absolute worst thing you can do is go back down there."

Staring right at Q, Picard tapped his combadge. "Picard to transporter room. Ensign Luptowski, an away team will be beaming down to Gorsach IX presently."

"Aye, sir."

Leaning down to whisper in Picard's ear, Worf could just hear Q's words: "Don't say I didn't warn you, *mon capitaine.*"

And with that, he disappeared.

"Captain," Worf said, relieved that Q had finally gone, "I did not wish to object in front of Q—or the admiral—but you cannot lead the away team."

"I can and I will, Number One," Picard said sternly. "The decision has been made." Then he added, "Under normal circumstances, Worf, your instinct would be the right one, but if Q is this desperate for us not to know what's down there, I *have* to see it for myself."

Worf considered pursuing the argument—and were it anyone other than Q, he would have—but he knew that it would be a wasted effort.

"As you say, sir. However, I must insist you bring a full security team."

Nodding, Picard said, "Agreed." He turned to look at the table. "Commander Kadohata, Lieutenant Leybenzon, you will both accompany me to the surface."

Kadohata nodded and said, "Aye, sir."

"Lieutenant, bring two of your people as well."

Leybenzon rose. "Sir, with respect, I would like to recommend a team of five."

"Your recommendation is noted, Lieutenant. However, a team of three will be sufficient."

"Aye, sir." If Leybenzon was disappointed, he didn't show it.

"We'll meet in Transporter Room 3 in twenty minutes. Dismissed." With that, Picard left the observation lounge, quickly followed by Crusher and T'Lana. Kadohata and La Forge gathered up their padds and departed moments later, leaving Worf and Leybenzon alone.

"Thank you, Commander," Leybenzon said, only now letting his irritation show. "If you hadn't insisted, he would probably have taken only me."

"Yes," Worf said. "The captain is sometimes blind to his own security needs. However, where Q is concerned—"

Shaking his head, Leybenzon said, "Yes, I know. I have read Starfleet reports about him, though I do not think I truly believed them."

Leybenzon looked frustrated. Worf could sympathize, as he'd gone through the same difficulties when he was in charge of security and Q showed up.

To Worf's amusement, Leybenzon asked, "Commander, how did you deal with it?"

"For the most part, I did not. Q cannot be dealt with, Lieutenant, he can only be . . . endured."

Leybenzon let out a noise that was part snort

and part laugh. "Well, fine, I endured Starbase 23, I can endure this." He tapped his combadge. "Leybenzon to security."

"Kapsis here."

"Ensign, who are the next two up on the duty roster?"

"Stolovitzky and de Lange."

Leybenzon nodded. "Good. Have them report to Transporter Room 3 for away duty immediately."

"Yes, sir."

Wasting no time, Leybenzon was moving toward the door.

"Lieutenant," Worf said, bringing Leybenzon up short.

"Yes?"

Worf hesitated, then spoke the words Will Riker had often said to him whenever Picard had insisted on leading away teams in the past. "Remember, your primary duty will be to protect the captain."

"Of course, Commander, worry not." He broke into a grin. "And afterward, we will share a bottle of Stolichnaya and you can tell me more stories of this Q fellow."

"Perhaps we shall," Worf said with a nod.

Leybenzon returned the nod and left the observation lounge.

14

—•—

Enterprise
In orbit of Gorsach IX

The day the universe ends

ZELIK LEYBENZON GENERALLY HAD VERY LITTLE
patience with officers, never mind the fact that he
was one—that wasn't his choice, after all. In fact,
the presence of so many officers was one of the reasons why Leybenzon considered turning down the
assignment to the *Enterprise.*

As part of the detail that had been overhauling
Starbase 23's security procedures, Leybenzon had
been serving as deputy chief under a less-than-
competent Bolian named Commander Aenni. Having had enough, he had requested a transfer to the

Bajoran sector. Leybenzon had been posted there before and during the war, and he wanted to go back. Unfortunately, none—Bajor, Deep Space 9, any of the nearby colonies, or even in Cardassian territory—had an opening for a junior-grade lieutenant in security.

And then he'd been summoned by Starbase 23's commander, Admiral Vance Haden. Leybenzon had even less use for admirals, but Haden was the exception. Indeed, Leybenzon had taken the starbase assignment because Haden was in command. It had been the admiral who put Leybenzon forward for a battlefield commission during the war—over the objections of the *Andromeda*'s CO.

The admiral, whose size was intimidating, was just staring at Zelik. Leybenzon wondered if something else had gone wrong with the security overhaul. He wondered if, once again, he was being assigned the blame. Three times before, when Aenni did something wrong, the Bolian had shifted the responsibility onto Leybenzon.

"I know you've put in for a transfer," Haden had finally said after staring at him unblinkingly. His hands were folded on his desk. The desk was free of decoration or personal accoutrements, like the man: no muss, no fuss.

"Yes, sir, I have."

"I can understand why. Honestly, I'm grateful you've stuck it out this long." Haden actually cracked a smile, something Leybenzon hadn't seen in his seven months serving on this starbase.

"Unfortunately, Aenni is a bear we have to cross."

Leybenzon ignored the admiral's deliberate malapropism. "Yes, sir."

"I was tempted to turn down your request, to be honest, but for selfish reasons. You've done a better job than his last three assistants fixing Aenni's snafus, and I don't want to lose you. However, you're in luck." Haden turned the computer station on his desk around so it faced Leybenzon. There was a standard officer posting request. "You seem to be desired by one Worf, son of Mogh."

At the sound of that name, Leybenzon had stood up straight. He'd worked with Worf a few times during the war, both at DS9 and when the *Andromeda* had been part of a joint Klingon-Federation strike force. They had both been raised on Gault, and Leybenzon had liked working with the Klingon. *Last I heard, he was Federation ambassador to the Klingons.* The embassy on Qo'noS had been attacked, and Leybenzon thought that Worf was requesting him for the security detail.

"What is it that Ambassador Worf wishes me to do?"

"Not 'ambassador' anymore, he's back in Starfleet and is the first officer of the *Enterprise.* Their security chief was killed, and *Commander* Worf specifically asked for you as the replacement."

That had caught Leybenzon off guard. The absolute last place he wanted to serve was on one of the frontline starships because most of their security people were officers. Leybenzon didn't trust any security detail that wasn't primarily enlisted personnel, and on the flagship, he'd be ass-deep in brass.

But it *was* the flagship. People stepped all over each other for the opportunity to serve under Jean-Luc Picard, to serve on the *Enterprise.*

"So," Haden said, "I guess you'll be packing."

"No," Leybenzon replied. "With all due respect, the *Enterprise* is not the ideal place for me."

"Are you out of your mind?" Haden leaned back and shook his head. "Zelik, this isn't the kind of opportunity that comes by very often. You turn it down, and I guarantee it won't come by again. What's more, nothing else will. Let me be frank, Zelik. Starbase 23 is the ass end of nowhere. That's why I asked to be assigned here. I've been in Starfleet longer than your parents have been alive, and after the war, I wanted something that would be a little less strenuous. Unfortunately, backwater starbases get the problem cases. Like Aenni. And you."

"I was not aware that I was a 'problem case,' Admiral."

"Which is part of why you are one. I've got reports from superiors of yours over the years, and they all say the same thing: 'Best security officer I ever had, but I don't ever want him serving under me again, under any circumstances.'" Haden leaned forward. "You piss people off, Zelik. You *know* that you piss people off. You don't *care* that you piss people off. That's why I asked for you. It was the only way you would ever get a favorable report from a CO. You've been here two years, and the only black marks are from Aenni. Command will consider the source; I've put nothing but praise in your jacket."

"I appreciate that, sir." Haden had been Leybenzon's rabbi, advocating his commission and running interference when Academy graduates got their backs up about him.

"But if you turn down an assignment to the *Enterprise,* you're done. That puts a label on your file that I won't be able to erase: that you don't take the opportunities handed to you. Zelik, you've been given a lifeline for your career by Commander Worf. If you don't take it, then I guarantee, you're gonna be cleaning up the messes of jackasses like Aenni for the rest of your career. You succeed with Picard, you can write your ticket after that."

As a general rule, Zelik Leybenzon had put advice from admirals in the same category as waste product. But Haden was the exception. "I accept, sir."

"Good, I'll get you transported today." The admiral shook his hand. "Dismissed."

Zelik had been hearing stories about the Rozhenkos' Klingon boy all of his life. The farming community on Gault was a very close-knit one. While the Rozhenkos had retired to Minsk on Earth by the time Leybenzon was a teenager, the stories about them lingered. Not all those stories were pleasant ones. Worf had accidentally caused the death of a fellow teenager during a soccer game. But by the time Leybenzon was old enough to be playing soccer, he assumed the stories about Worf had grown with the retelling. When they met on DS9, Leybenzon was impressed with Worf's professionalism. Serving with him would be a great privilege.

He had attempted to use Haden's advice. When La Forge had joined Leybenzon and the people in the Riding Club, his first instinct had been to tell the chief engineer to leave. But he recalled Haden's words about pissing people off. While Leybenzon generally had even less use for engineers than he did officers—never mind someone who was both—he also knew that being disrespectful to a superior officer was wrong.

What surprised Leybenzon was that he found that La Forge was good company. He didn't put on the airs that Leybenzon had come to expect from high-ranking types but acted as if they were all equals. The story he told was entertaining. He doubted he'd ever consider Geordi La Forge a close friend, but he also was willing to put him in the same category as Haden and Worf: officers he could tolerate.

The real difficulty was the one he'd anticipated before arriving: an officer-filled security team was nowhere near up to snuff. The ones that were left from Battaglia's brief tenure were slow, barely fit, and far below the standards that Leybenzon expected. The exceptions were people Leybenzon himself had requested.

Two exceptions were in the transporter room with

Leybenzon and Kadohata: Natasha Stolovitzky and Harley de Lange. Stolovitzky had been an enlisted grunt serving alongside Leybenzon on the *Andromeda*. He had recommended her for the *Roosevelt* when he was assigned there after the war, only to discover that she had been accepted to the Academy. Once on *Enterprise*, Leybenzon poached her from Deep Space 3 and made her his deputy chief.

De Lange had been another of the "problem cases" of Starbase 23, showing tendencies toward insubordination and recalcitrance. The young man, who was a mix of several Earth nationalities, had an odd-featured face and a small, compact body. Leybenzon put him in his own squad and whipped him into shape. Leybenzon had asked Haden to allow him to take de Lange with him to the *Enterprise*.

Worf and the captain arrived. The second officer snapped her tricorder shut. "Ready when you are, sir."

Picard said, "Let us proceed."

The captain stepped up to the transporter. Leybenzon waited until Kadohata had joined Picard before proceeding to his own pad. Stolovitzky and de Lange were seconds behind Leybenzon.

Worf nodded his approval.

Leybenzon ordered, "On stun." He saw no reason to be caught unawares and had never agreed with the policy of leaving weapons holstered during beamdown, especially when the location was likely to be hostile.

"Take care, Worf, with Q you never know."

"Understood, sir."

"Energize, Ensign," Picard ordered.

The canyon was warmer than it had been, and a heavy breeze blew through Leybenzon's thin brown hair, but there was no sign of the predators.

Kadohata reported, "I'm reading no life signs, aside from the lower life-forms we encountered the last time."

Leybenzon lowered his weapon but did not holster it. After all, they hadn't detected the predators last time. He took up position near Picard.

Pointing to one of the cavern openings, Kadohata said, "It's this way, sir." Leybenzon was grateful. He did not recall which was which—the openings all looked alike in the perfect symmetry of this canyon.

Leybenzon pointed two fingers at de Lange and three at Stolovitzky, and they both nodded. The lieutenant took point, moving toward the cavern with Picard, Kadohata, and de Lange, Stolovitzky covering the rear.

At the mouth of the cavern, Leybenzon stopped and took out his own tricorder. He detected the same mineral composition in the cavern walls he did the last time and nothing else aside from a thirty-meter-long twisting path.

Kadohata confirmed that. "Not picking up anything unusual, Captain."

Picard nodded. "Not surprising. Proceed, Lieutenant."

"Aye, sir." Leybenzon put his tricorder away and slowly walked into the cavern, phaser raised.

Just like last time, Leybenzon found himself unable to move forward after he reached the ten-meter mark. This time he summoned up every erg of willpower he had and tried to lift his left foot.

Nothing.

"Perhaps if we all try at once," Kadohata said.

Leybenzon turned to look at her. "Sir?"

"Last time, each of us tried individually. What if all five of us try to walk through at once?"

With a shrug, Leybenzon looked to the captain.

"Make it so," Picard said with a nod.

All five officers then stood abreast in the tight confines of the cavern and stepped forward.

Suddenly, Leybenzon felt his stomach drop, like he was on a g-coaster, and he tried to scream—

—out to his troops, "Firm up! Don't let those Jem'Hadar bastards break the line!"

The trenches of Chin'toka IX had gotten muddy in the rain, but Zelik Leybenzon wasn't overly concerned. All they had to do was defend the installation on the ground. The Jem'Hadar couldn't just bombard the place from orbit because there was a Founder in the installation's brig, and the Jem'Hadar wouldn't vaporize one of their gods.

So they were attacking on the ground, hiding behind the tree line and taking their shots, slowly moving forward toward the trenches the Starfleet soldiers had dug in front of the installation. Zelik had hoped he'd be able to outlast the Jem'Hadar, but there seemed to be an endless supply of them, where he had only a hundred troops left. Thirty-four had been fatally wounded.

Zelik had always found the Jem'Hadar and Vorta's slavish devotion to the Founders to be their weak spot. Now it was the reason Starfleet even had a chance to secure Chin'toka IX. Of course, it also painted a big target on the planet, as the Jem'Hadar would stop at nothing to retrieve their god. Zelik was a good soldier. He was ordered to hold this installation, so that was what he was doing.

The only thing Zelik had ever really believed in was himself and his skills with weaponry. He trusted nothing and nobody else.

Not even the people under him, which was as it should be, because they weren't doing as he asked. "I said, firm *up*!" There were seven holes in the line that the Jem'Hadar could exploit.

Phaser fire whined over his head, and Zelik cursed the incompetents that Starfleet had been sending him lately. Getting experienced ground troops had become increasingly difficult. As year five ground into year six, with no obvious end in sight, the troops got greener and greener. The cost in lives was appalling, but it was far better than the alternative. Zelik had seen what the Dominion had done to Betazed, reducing a once-great world to a wasteland, and he would die before he saw that happen to another Federation world.

Or, rather, he'd kill to prevent it.

From his right, Deng said, "Sir, the Jem'Hadar have deactivated the proximity grenades!"

Zelik noted the panic in the young soldier's voice, but simply nodded and said, "Okay."

"Okay? Sir, we were counting on those grenades to—"

Suddenly half the trees exploded. Grinning wolfishly as he heard the death screams of dozens of Jem'Hadar, Zelik cried, "Weapons free—fire on them, *now!*"

The troops opened fire into the conflagration, resulting in still more oh-so-satisfying agonized wails of dying Jem'Hadar. Zelik lived for that sound.

Deng looked at him in openmouthed shock. "How—?"

"Programmed the grenades in the trees to stay inactive and cloaked until the grenades in the ground were deactivated."

"At which point they activate and detonate?" Deng smiled. "You're amazing, sir."

"Don't be stupid. I'm just a soldier doing his duty—do not forget that. And keep firing."

Zelik settled into the rhythm of firing his phaser rifle, watching the amber beams issue forth and cut into the Jem'Hadar's scaly flesh. Something at the back of his head whispered to him: Pak-Cho Deng had died on the *Andromeda*. Ridiculous. Deng was right there next to him, killing Jem'Hadar.

Smiling contentedly as he took down another

Jem'Hadar, Zelik Leybenzon thought, *This is the way it was meant to be. . . .*

Ensign Natasha Stolovitzky moved forward from her position to stand next to Captain Picard. She had been surprised that the captain was leading this landing party. She realized the presence of Q made it obvious that there was more to this entire mission than met the eye. Natasha had studied the reports of his appearances and was not looking forward to how the mission was likely to progress.

Still, she would do her best for Lieutenant Leybenzon. Besides, he always told the best stories. . . .

Suddenly, Stolovitzky felt her stomach turn inside out, and she tried to scream—

—out her brother's name: "Sebastian! Where *are* you?"

"Over here!"

Natasha traced the sound of her brother's voice to the big weeping willow tree behind the house.

"What're you doing?"

"I found a gecko!"

She rolled her eyes. Sebastian had a fascination with amphibians and lizards that dated back to when they were both children. "It's time for dinner!"

The one thing that could tear Sebastian away was the promise of food. "Coming!"

They went inside together and sat at the table,

where the replicated lamb stew and six-cheese risotto sat waiting for them. Natasha had experimented and programmed the replicator to make the risotto with mozzarella, Wensleydale, Irish cheddar, Gouda, *trwoqa* cheese from Canopus, and her personal favorite, *lemto* from Ferenginar.

As they ate, Sebastian asked, "How's the novel coming?"

Natasha shuddered. "Don't ask. I wrote myself into another corner with Nyzik. I can't think of a good reason why he'd go on the mission."

Sebastian shook his head as he swallowed some stew. "I told you making your protagonist a person with no morals would get you in trouble."

"Yeah, yeah." Natasha sighed. "I knew fiction was a mistake. I'm going to talk to Thea about doing another travel book."

Sebastian scooped up some risotto with his fork and ate it, then almost immediately spit it out. "You put one of the Ferengi cheeses in here, didn't you?"

"Er, well—"

"You *know* I can't stand that stuff. Jeez, Natasha! I'm gonna get something *decent* from the replicator."

Even as she laughed at her brother, Natasha had an odd feeling, like the fact that she hadn't set foot in this house since she enlisted in Starfleet seven years ago. But that was ridiculous—Natasha had never joined Starfleet. Why should she, with her career as a writer doing so well?

Smiling contentedly as she ate, Natasha

Stolovitzky thought, *This is the way it was meant to be. . . .*

As he moved from the rear of the line to stand next to Stolovitzky, Ensign Harley de Lange found himself eagerly wondering what was going to happen next. Three months ago, he'd been convinced that his career was at an end. Thanks to Lieutenant Leybenzon, de Lange was serving on the *Enterprise*. This had been a dream come true for him, ever since he was a boy living on Earth looking up at the stars.

Suddenly, de Lange felt his stomach churn madly, like that time he made the mistake of drinking some of Leybenzon's vodka, and he tried to scream—

—out, "Come on, you stupid pile of bolts, *climb!*"

The client had told Harley de Lange that she needed him to make a pickup on Dorcas. What she *hadn't* told Harley was that there had been a coup d'état on Dorcas, and that the new subjugator was not favorably disposed to the Federation and had cast out all Federation diplomatic personnel and citizens.

At least the subjugator's personal navy had only high-powered lasers, but Harley's ship's shields weren't what you'd call state of the art. Sooner or later, the lasers were going to burn through, and then he'd be royally cooked. His ship wasn't affiliated with the Federation, but as soon as the Dorca learned he was human, all bets were off.

He'd managed to get to his ship, having already transported the cargo on board, but he had to get out of orbit so he could go to warp. The Dorca hadn't yet achieved faster-than-light travel, so as soon as Harley was clear of the planet, the navy would be eating his space dust.

Assuming, of course, he made it that far.

He checked the navigation computer and saw that he'd be clear of the atmosphere in two minutes.

This is gonna be a long two minutes.

If he had a Starfleet shuttle, he wouldn't have this problem. *Why did I think that?* he wondered. Harley had never even thought about joining Starfleet.

Smiling contentedly as his ship started to clear the stratosphere, Harley de Lange thought, *This is the way it was meant to be. . . .*

God, I missed this, Lieutenant Commander Miranda Kadohata thought as she stepped forward in a line with the rest of the away team. Not that she regretted the decision to have Colin and Sylvana, but being on maternity leave had been agonizing for her. She didn't realize how much until she was back. Standing on an alien world, wondering what its secret was—*this* was why Miranda joined Starfleet.

Holding up her tricorder, she stepped forward with the others hoping to pass through the invisible threshold that separated this part of the cavern from what they found with the MRI and X-rays.

Suddenly, Kadohata felt her stomach heave with a blinding agony that reminded her of the worst elements of giving birth, and she tried to scream—

—in frustration as the student gave the wrong answer. *I swear, there are times when I think the admissions standards have been dumbed down to the point where single-cell paramecia could get into this blasted university.*

Professor Miranda Kadohata, Ph.D., knew that wasn't fair, and that Bacco University had excellent admissions standards. But it insisted that all students take at least one general sciences class in their first two years, and it also required that every science professor employed by the university teach at least one of the required classes each semester.

In theory, Miranda approved of the notion. After all, every student should get a well-rounded education. In practice, she found herself teaching an astrophysics class to people who wanted to be anything *but* astrophysicists.

Case in point: Gar Tarklem, the young Trill in the front row, who was planning to get his degree in history. He'd just said in front of the entire class that comets have consistent orbits.

"Gar, comets aren't overburdened with a huge mass, therefore their orbits can be changed by proximity to a body that *does* have mass, like an asteroid, a planet, or a sun." Miranda prayed for the class to end.

Another student, a human woman named Ariana Rodriguez, raised her hand. "Or a starship, yes?"

Miranda nodded. "It would depend on the ship. Something large and slow might attract the comet, but modern craft are prepared to handle that." She smiled. "The older colony ships would've had a bit more trouble."

She continued about comets for the rest of the hour. Miraculously, no one else made any stupid comments.

Afterward, a few students came up to her with questions, all of which she answered in quick succession. "No, I won't postpone the midterm. Yes, both chapters by Friday. I wouldn't trust Viksash as a source, a lot of his theories were shot down after the exploration of the Xintil Nebula." She then escaped to her office.

There were a dozen messages on her workstation, departmental bulletins, university bulletins, or notes from students. She intended to read the student notes first, but there was also a text-only message from T'Vorak, the chair of the astrophysics department: CONTACT ME IMMEDIATELY.

Miranda's heart was racing. *Could it be?* It had been so long since she'd submitted the grant application, she had all but assumed that it had been turned down.

Miranda put through a communication to the

department head. Within ten seconds, the angular features of T'Vorak appeared on her workstation's screen.

"Doctor Kadohata, I have news that I believe you will find satisfactory," T'Vorak said.

Her heart raced faster. "The grant came through?"

T'Vorak's right eyebrow rose. *"Indeed. Were you informed?"*

Laughing, Miranda said, "No, merely a fervent hope. Oh, T'Vorak, this is wonderful news!"

"I expected you to react in such a manner." T'Vorak looked away briefly to touch some controls on her workstation. *"I am forwarding the specifics to you now. The expedition's departure date was delayed; therefore, you will be able to complete this semester's work. Because of that delay, they have been forced to switch to a smaller vessel."*

Miranda didn't like the sound of that. "What does that mean, exactly?"

"Families will not be permitted."

Nodding, Miranda said, "Thank you, T'Vorak. I'll look at the file now."

After T'Vorak's face disappeared from the screen, Miranda let out a long breath. The expedition to the Ventax system was the chance of a lifetime, as Ventax's solar flares were unique. Starfleet had constructed a base on the outskirts of the system, and Miranda had applied to be one of the civilian scientists. *It's another chance to stand on an alien world and explore the unknown.*

That thought brought her up short. *"Another"* *chance? I've never been off Cestus. Odd.*

The application had said that families could come. Apparently, that was no longer the case.

What does it matter? All your shipboard assignments have taken you away from home. Vicenzo knew that when he met you.

Miranda blinked. *Where did that thought come from?*

Yet a part of her mind insisted that this was wrong, that she'd spent all her adult life on starships, exploring new worlds—that she'd set foot on *dozens* of alien worlds.

But that's absurd. I've lived on Cestus all my life, with Vicenzo and Aoki and the twins. We met after—

Her mind seemed conflicted. Being in this office, applying for this grant, teaching at this university— all of it was just *wrong* somehow.

Leaning back in her chair, Doctor Miranda Kadohata wondered, *Is this really the way it was meant to be?*

Captain Jean-Luc Picard took a deep breath before stepping forward with the rest of his landing party.

He knew that his assuming command was probably foolhardy. That he was able to do so by counting on Worf's unswerving loyalty and belief in his captain made Picard feel bad. However, he couldn't just sit around waiting to see what would happen.

Not with Q involved.

Picard understood and accepted Starfleet regulations that required captains to put their own safety above all others'. He had been known to bend those rules when circumstances required. Q was a circumstance that required his direct intervention. For one thing, Q almost always dragged Picard into whatever game he was playing.

So I might as well insert myself before Q has the chance to.

As he joined his people in moving forward, he suddenly felt something horribly painful in his stomach, and he tried to scream—

—but his voice caught in his throat.

What is this place?

It took him a moment to orient himself on the uneven ground of the dig site. He waved his arms to steady himself in the thick work boots and managed to regain his balance.

"Are you all right, Jean-Luc?"

He turned around to see Professor Galen looking at him with a concerned expression. "Yes," he said after a moment, "I'm fine, I just—" For several seconds, Jean-Luc tried to figure out where he was. *I'm at the dig site, of course. Professor Galen and I—*

Cutting the thought off, he looked again at Galen. "What are you doing here?"

Laughing tersely, the professor said, "Where else would you expect me to be, Jean-Luc? Now come on, we have a lot of digging to do before the sun sets. And then we get to spend the night cataloging."

"No," Jean-Luc said quietly.

"I beg your pardon?" Galen asked in that imperious voice of his.

Looking around, Jean-Luc saw that they were in a deep recess in the ground of some planet or other. *We're on Phnadrux,* his mind suddenly said, *exploring the Phnodra ruins.* But that was impossible.

He looked down, seeing the work boots he'd felt weighing his feet down, and the earth-toned civilian clothes he was wearing. *"Civilian clothes"? What a ridiculous notion—these are the clothes I always wear, and I've been a civilian all my life.*

But it was wrong. Picard *knew* this was wrong.

Nonsense, it's as real as—

As what?

Now Galen sounded concerned. "Jean-Luc, are you feeling all right?"

"I'm fine," he said with what he hoped was a reassuring smile. Making a show of wiping some sweat off his face, he said, "The sun's just gotten to me a bit."

Galen chuckled. "You used to have better stamina than that, Jean-Luc."

"Look who's talking, old man," Picard said, returning the chuckle. "I believe the expression is 'Eat my dust.'"

"That's the spirit, Jean-Luc." Galen put an encouraging hand on Picard's arm and then moved on down the dig site.

As soon as he was immersed in his own section of the dig, Jean-Luc looked up. *Something's wrong. Richard Galen is dead. He died eleven years ago on the* Enterprise *after those Yridians attacked him.*

"No," he muttered to himself. "It can't be. This is reality, this dig site. It's *real,* dammit, as real as—"

Galen called from down the dig site. "You say something, Jean-Luc?"

"Just talking to myself, Professor," he yelled back. Then, with a small smile, he added, "It's my only guarantee of intelligent conversation."

"Very droll, Jean-Luc. If there were two of you, you'd make one whole wit!"

The banter between them was comfortable, the good-natured jibes of two men who had once been mentor and student and now were peers, having worked together for decades.

No, he's been dead for eleven years—and we never worked together. I graduated the Academy and went on to—

To what? Why couldn't he remember?

He looked down at the relics that he and the professor had unearthed, including one piece of pottery that looked like it came from the Byrlax period. *No, wait, it has the representation of the god of the harvest, and that means it has to be from the Torgox period.*

Reaching down, he picked up the pottery shard and examined it. The hard clay felt real in his hand. And yet, it could not be real.

This is wrong. Yet this is right.

Instinctively, he focused on the pottery shard. Studied the intricacy of the etchings in the clay, the swirls and angles that represented how the Phnodra portrayed the god of the harvest. Lost himself in the artistry, the passion of the worship and fealty that the long-dead Phnodra had for their harvest god.

Made it a perfect moment in time.

Everything slowed to a crawl. The gentle breeze all but stopped. It was just as Anij had taught him; Jean-Luc Picard heard her voice.

He focused on the pottery shard—

—which wasn't there. It was a rock in a cave on Gorsach IX.

Standing up, Jean-Luc Picard realized that this was *not* the way it was meant to be.

And then the world exploded.

15

———

Somewhere . . .

JEAN-LUC PICARD FOUND HIMSELF STANDING IN A
bright room.

No, not a room. A pure white space. A place that
was both everywhere and nowhere.

He had been here before.

Once again, he called out to the one who simply
had to be responsible for this, especially since *he*
was the one who'd brought Picard here the last
time, under the guise of it being the afterlife.

"Q! Show yourself!"

"Of course, Jean-Luc."

Picard turned around to see Q, dressed in the
same white robes he had fashioned for himself
when he'd brought Picard here more than a decade

ago, after the Lenarians almost killed him. "What is this all about, Q?"

"All about? Quite simply, Jean-Luc, this is the most important moment of your misbegotten life."

"Enough! No more riddles, Q, no more word games. Tell me what is happening."

Sighing dramatically, Q said, "Calm down, Jean-Luc. My intention is to explain everything, now that you've gotten the ball rolling, as it were."

"What ball? What are you—"

"—talking about? I'd be happy to explain. All it requires is that you not interrupt."

Picard tugged his uniform jacket downward and gazed expectantly at Q.

Smiling, Q said, "That's better." He started to pace around Picard as he spoke, gesticulating a bit as he went. "Gorsach IX, as you call it—and where did you come up with such a dreadful name, anyhow?" Before Picard could answer, Q waved him off. "But that's neither here nor there. The point is, that planet is not what it appears to be."

"Obviously," Picard said dryly.

Q stopped pacing. "What did I say about interrupting?"

Resisting the urge to speak, Picard simply stared at Q.

Resuming his pacing, Q said, "The planet is a construct that is protecting what you have just unleashed by walking into that cavern: the end of the universe. I have been spending the last few moments—what you would term as about sixteen years—manipulating humanity so that they would reach this place at this time and stop the universe from ceasing to exist."

"That's absurd! You haven't been manipulating anything, you've simply come in and—"

"Tested you. Put you in the path of the Borg. Expanded your horizons in terms of understanding the meaning of time and space. All of that, Jean-Luc, and more, has been in the service of getting you to this place now. If it hadn't been you, it might well have been the Borg. That is why you needed to encounter them sooner, so you could stymie them—and so Kathy and her band of nitwits would be armed with the knowledge to devastate them to the point that they'd never get here." Q actually shuddered then. "Trust me, Jean-Luc, you don't want to imagine the consequences to the universe if the Borg found this place before you did."

"But what *is* this place? What is Gorsach IX?"

"Weren't you listening?" Q snapped. "It's a construct that holds back entropy, that keeps the universe from collapsing in on itself."

"How is it possible? One planet cannot keep the galaxy—"

"Universe, Jean-Luc, not galaxy. In other words, *all* the galaxies are at stake here. Really, if you don't start paying attention—"

"Then say something that makes sense, Q!"

Q stopped pacing. "Very well. To put this into metaphorical language that your tiny mind can comprehend, Gorsach IX is the stopper in the drain. By penetrating the illusion of the cavern—"

"That wasn't you?"

Another sigh. *"Must* you keep interrupting? No, that wasn't me, that was the planet's defense system, for lack of a better term. It sent each of you to someplace where you lived out your life as someone who never would've come near Gorsach IX. The newt was fighting an endless war, his two grunts were living lives so boring that no one could care, and dear Randy was back on Cestus III. You and Randy were the only ones who even had an inkling that it was an illusion, and you're the only one who penetrated it. Nicely done, by the way—I didn't think any humans had picked up that trick."

Under other circumstances, Picard might have taken some comfort from his being able to surprise Q with the lessons he'd learned from the Ba'ku. But he was still somewhat taken aback by how intense and serious Q was being under his trademark snideness. "So what happens now?"

"I told you, the universe comes to an end. This planet was holding back the chain reaction that would wipe it all out. Now that the illusion has been shattered, fissures in space are opening all throughout the universe. Those rifts that dear Kathy told you about are only the beginning."

Befuddlement was now giving way to anger, which was certainly a more familiar emotion where Q was concerned. "Dammit, Q, why didn't you just come out and *say* something?"

Q started pacing again. "Isn't it obvious? Because you wouldn't have believed me, Jean-Luc. The best way to get you to go into that cavern was to tell you that you shouldn't. Millennia of evolution, and still humans are subject to that most basic of concepts, reverse psychology."

Picard rubbed the bridge of his nose between his thumb and forefinger. "Yes, Q, I understand that—"

"Will wonders never cease," Q muttered.

"—but why have me go into the cavern in the *first* place if all it would do is destroy the universe?"

Q stopped and stood facing Picard. "Because, Jean-Luc, it's a necessary part of the process. There's only one way to stop the drain backup, to beat the metaphor into the ground. And only *you* can do it." Again, he started to pace. "The arguments over this have nearly torn the Continuum apart. We fought a civil war, you know."

"Yes, I've read Admiral Janeway's reports."

"Of course you did. The little antebellum fantasy she described was just her own interpretation of it. It was a terrible conflict, one that nearly did Gorsach IX's job for it."

Picard folded his arms again. "And you saved the day by having a child."

"Yes. No need to thank me—believe me, q is thanks enough," Q said with more than a little sarcasm. "In any event, I was convinced that you were the ones to find this place and do what needed to be done. The other Q were less sure, viewing you— not without reason, I might add—as a bunch of delusional bipeds with little hope of understanding the basics of reality, much less saving the universe."

Regarding Q skeptically, Picard said, "Are you saying that . . . *you* were humanity's advocate?"

Smirking, Q said, "Ironic, isn't it?"

"Q, I still don't understand—"

"And now he doesn't understand," Q said while looking up, though from whom Q would ask supplication Picard didn't dare contemplate. "Would that he would make up his mind."

"What is my role in this?"

Q smiled. "Oh, that's simple, Jean-Luc. You have to be yourself."

With that, Q snapped his fingers, and Picard disappeared.

16

—

Enterprise
Gorsach system

The end of the universe

"COMMANDER," ENSIGN BALIDEMAJ SAID FROM tactical, "Gorsach IX has disappeared."

From the conn, Lieutenant Faur said, "Confirmed. The planet's just . . . just gone."

Worf rose from the captain's chair. "Red Alert. Hail the away team."

Balidemaj operated her console even as the Red Alert siren went off and the lighting dimmed. The entire bridge was now cast in a red glow. Balidemaj looked up, giving Worf a stricken look. "I'm sorry, sir, but—"

Tapping his combadge, the first officer said, "Worf to transporter room. Ensign Luptowski, beam up the away team."

"Stand by—sir, I've lost the lock on them. In fact, uhm—I've lost the planet."

Turning to Lieutenant Rosado at ops, Worf said, "Sensors?"

Shaking her head, Rosado said, "I'm checking the sensors now, sir, but . . . well, they're not picking up anything."

At that moment, Kadohata, Leybenzon, Stolovitzky, and de Lange appeared on the bridge. There was no transporter effect, not even the glow that often accompanied one of Q's tricks. One moment they weren't there; the next, they were.

All four of them looked disoriented.

"Stations!" Worf barked, and that got them all moving.

Leybenzon quickly assumed tactical, Stolovitzky and de Lange left for their Red Alert stations. Worf put a hand on Miranda's shoulder before she could go to ops. "Where is the captain?"

"Commander, I don't even know what *I'm* doing here. Last thing I remember, we were all in the cavern, then—" She had a faraway look for a moment, then stared hard at Worf. "I'm sorry."

"Take your station," Worf said, letting her go.

Kadohata took a reading. "Sir, there's something coming in from the probes in orbit of Gorsach V." She looked up. "You'll never believe this, but it looks like it's about to ignite into a red dwarf!"

From tactical, Leybenzon said, "That should take centuries."

"I know—it normally does."

From the bridge engineering station, La Forge pointed out, "There is nothing 'normal' whenever Q's around."

Worf sat back in the command chair. "Put the fifth planet on screen. Continue scanning for the captain, and—" Worf cut himself off at the sight of the fifth planet. It was igniting, all right, but not turning into a sun. The planet collapsed in on itself, giving off a huge burst of energy. "Shields!"

"Full power," said Leybenzon from behind him.

Worf stared at the viewscreen. Gorsach V was now half the size it had been only a moment before. What unfolded before him was Gorsach V going through a similar process that should, as Kadohata had indicated, take centuries occurring in only a few minutes.

A flash of light, and the star exploded outward again. "Shields holding," Leybenzon said.

From ops, Kadohata reported, "Continuing sensor scans, but I'm finding no signs of the captain's combadge—or any life signs anywhere in this system outside the *Enterprise*."

Worf heard a hand slamming on the tactical console. "How can a planet disappear like this?" Leybenzon asked.

Kadohata's fingers danced over the controls as if something, anything, she could do would find the captain. The Klingon got up, drawn into the horror unfolding on the viewscreen. Standing beside Miranda, Worf heard her mumble, "The same way we got transported back here from whatever fantasyland Q sent us to."

"Fantasyland?" Worf asked. He trailed off. Gorsach V was indeed collapsing, but it was not becoming a red dwarf. Worf looked down at the readouts on the ops console.

"Sir, the readings from Gorsach V aren't tracking with a gas giant collapsing into a red dwarf. In fact, I don't know what to make of this," Kadohata reported.

Worf knew.

It was becoming a blue-white mass of swirling energy approximately a quarter of the diameter that the gas giant had been.

"It's some kind of fissure," Kadohata said. "I don't recognize the type, and the database is coming up empty."

"It is a quantum fissure in the space-time continuum," Worf calmly stated.

Kadohata said, "Sir?"

"I have encountered the phenomenon before."

"Due respect, sir, why isn't it in the database?"

Worf explained, "If you examine the log entries I made on stardate 47391, you will see a reference."

On his way back to the *Enterprise* from a *bat'leth* tournament, Worf's shuttle had passed through a fissure much like this one—it had sent him on a journey through half a dozen parallel universes. Unfortunately, the solution to the problem had meant that there were no visual records, no scans, just Worf's memory.

"Lieutenant Faur, bring us to within one hundred thousand kilometers of the quantum fissure, full impulse," Worf ordered.

"Aye, sir."

"Lieutenant Leybenzon, maintain Red Alert, shields at maximum."

"Aye, aye sir." Leybenzon asked, "What about the captain?"

Sitting back in the command chair, Worf said, "I suspect that he is in Q's hands."

Unhappily, Leybenzon said, "Aye, sir."

The quantum fissure was something Worf knew—and something he was uniquely qualified to handle.

"I'm reading something weird," La Forge reported. "The fissure's fluctuating."

A ship appeared near the fissure. Then another, and another.

"Report!" Worf said, striding to stand between Kadohata and Faur.

"There are dozens of ships appearing—most appear to be *Sovereign*-class." Leybenzon looked up, a perturbed expression on his face. "Sir, there aren't this many *Sovereign*-class ships in the fleet."

Kadohata said, "Commander, each of those ships is holding station at thirty thousand kilometers from the event horizon of the . . . the fissure."

"The same distance as us," Worf said.

"Aye, sir."

"Commander Kadohata, scan the other vessels for their quantum signatures."

Kadohata looked up at Worf. "Sir?"

"Obey my orders, Commander."

"Aye, sir." Kadohata quickly moved to obey.

Worf understood her confusion. Scanning for a quantum signature must have seemed like a waste of time, because all matter and energy in the universe had the exact same quantum signature.

If Worf was right, these ships were *not* from this universe.

"This isn't possible," Kadohata said with an incredulous tone. "Each of those ships has a *different* quantum signature."

"I get no IDs for the ships, but the visual registry numbers that I am able to decipher are the same." Leybenzon looked up. "Those ships are all the *Enterprise*."

"As I expected," Worf stated.

Kadohata was staring at him. "How?"

Leybenzon cried out, "One of the ships is firing on us!"

17

———

Quantum fissure, Gorsach system

The end of the universe

JEAN-LUC PICARD SAT ON THE BRIDGE OF THE
U.S.S. Enterprise.

To his right was an untried first officer; to his
left, a new counselor. As they faced this bizarre circumstance, he wondered how this crew might handle it. They had all been devastated by Data's death
at the hands of Shinzon, and then Riker and Troi
had gone on to the *Titan.*

Turning to his first officer, he said, "Number
One, what do you make of this?"

Commander Martin Madden leaned forward in
the first officer's chair, studying the viewscreen

with its multiple *Sovereign*-class ships all appearing around a rift. "I don't know what to make of it, Jea—er, Captain."

Picard sighed. Madden had been told by Riker that the captain preferred to be called by his first name, a practical joke that had surprised Picard and embarrassed the hell out of Madden.

"Counselor Hedril, do you sense anything?"

The young Cairn woman said, "There's a great deal of confusion, sir." She turned to Picard. "And with you, sir."

The captain realized that this was wrong. Hedril, who had visited the *Enterprise*-D as a girl, wasn't in Starfleet, and Picard had never heard of any Commander Martin Madden. The last thing he remembered was being in that all-white space with Q.

What the—

Jean-Luc Picard sat on the bridge of the *F.S.S. Enterprise.*

To his right was his trusted first officer of many years' standing; to his left, a new counselor. As they faced this bizarre new circumstance, he had every faith in his crew's ability to handle it. Ever since Data had advanced to the first officer's position—following Riker assuming command of the *Aries* a decade and a half ago—they had become the proverbial well-oiled machine.

Picard had gone through a variety of counselors since Troi had married and moved to Qo'noS to join her husband, Worf, the Federation ambassador to the Klingon Empire. None, though, had been able to replace Troi. He hoped that T'Lana would.

"Captain," Commander Data said, "I believe that what we have encountered is a quantum fissure across time and space. Each *Enterprise* that we are seeing is likely from a different quantum universe."

Picard nodded. To ops, he asked, "Commander Kadohata, can you verify that?"

From the operations console, Commander Geordi La Forge, his second, turned around and asked, "Captain?"

Picard realized that this was wrong, that La Forge should be in engineering, Worf should be by his side, and Data should be dead. The last thing he remembered was being with Q in that all-white area—and then somewhere else. But where?

What the hell—

Jean-Luc Picard sat on the bridge of the *U.S.V. Enterprise.*

He was alone, of course. Humans had long since engineered themselves to the point where the entire concept of a ship's crew was outmoded. The ship was hardwired directly into Picard's cranium, allowing him to more efficiently control ship's functions. He sat in the center of the bridge, connections to each station linked to a central machine behind him. The machine itself was integrated with Picard's skull. A separate machine to his right provided him with whatever nutrients he needed to survive, and another to the left monitored his health. If he became overly fatigued, another machine would sedate him until he was sufficiently rested to continue functioning.

Upon the ship's sudden appearance in this strange place, surrounded by dozens of similar ships, Picard accessed computer records. He got a hit on parallel universes and the theory that there were an infinite number of quantum universes, each with a distinctive signature. Picard had sensors scan the other vessels, and each one displayed a different quantum signature—which was impossible, as *everything* had the same signature. The only way this was possible was if the barriers between universes were breaking down.

But this is impossible! Picard thought, and not just about the quantum realities. He had a crew, not this . . . this Borg-like setup. He had been on two other *Enterprises*, and before that, he was with Q.

What the hell is—

Jean-Luc Picard sat on the bridge of the *U.S. Enterprise*.

To his left was the captain to whom he proudly served as first officer. True, Captain Wesley Crusher was much younger than his first officer, but Picard's lengthy career in the sciences had meant a slow promotion track for him—he'd gone into command only when his work on the survey of

Selcundi Drema brought him to the attention of Captain Jellico, who eventually made him second officer. After Data's death at the hands of the Reman usurper Vkruk, Picard became first officer— serving under the newest captain of the *Enterprise* and the son of his best friend.

Jack would be proud of what Wes has accomplished.

"Analysis, Miranda," Captain Crusher said to Lieutenant Kadohata at ops.

"Each of those ships is reading as a *Sovereign*-class ship—or as close as makes no never mind." She turned around. "Captain, some of these are IDing as the *Enterprise*."

Without even thinking about it, Picard ordered, "Commander, scan each of the other ships for its quantum signature."

Crusher turned to his first officer. "What are you thinking, Jean-Luc?"

For some reason, even though the captain always referred to his officers by first name, hearing Wesley Crusher say "Jean-Luc" sounded strange. Still and all, Picard explained himself. "I believe that these vessels are all from different quantum realities, that the phenomenon we're seeing in the center of all this is a quantum fissure."

An enthusiastic smile lit Crusher's face. "Parallel universe theory? That sure takes me back." He ordered Kadohata, "Do it, Miranda."

But Lieutenant Commander Jean-Luc Picard knew something was wrong. He knew about this from what he had learned on the *Enterprise*. Or, rather, the other *Enterprises*—which didn't make any sense. And what about Q?

What the hell is going—

Jean-Luc Picard sat on the bridge of the *I.S.S. Enterprise.*

To his right was his first officer. Lore had served efficiently, if not always faithfully, in the role ever since the ambitious android assassinated Riker. They had been on their way back to Earth to bring tribute to the empress when they came across this strange phenomenon.

From behind him, Chief Engineer Miles O'Brien said, "There's an odd quantum signature in all the matter around us, sir."

"Analysis, Mister O'Brien," Lore said.

"I don't know what to make of it, sir. Everything in the universe should have the same quantum signature. There's no way this could be happening."

Lore stood up to face the engineer at his aft console. "Oh, you'd better *find* a way, O'Brien. Otherwise, we'll just have to see how Mister Barclay likes being chief engineer." And then the android touched a control on his belt.

"Auuuuuugggggghhhhh!" O'Brien collapsed to his knees as the agonizer that was implanted in the base of his skull activated. Picard had implanted the devices in all of his officers' skulls—except for

Lore, who didn't have a nervous system. But Picard had other methods of dealing with Lore if the android ever got delusions of grandeur.

O'Brien slowly clambered to his feet when Lore was finished. "Of . . . of course, sir. I'll . . . I'll figure it out."

The captain said nothing—he left personnel items to Lore—however, he was expecting to see Geordi La Forge as chief engineer. *No, La Forge was born blind—he'd have been killed in this universe.*

"This" universe—that was not a construction he should have been using.

But he was. This was only the latest *Enterprise* he'd visited—and by far the least pleasant. Q had to have been doing this to him.

What the hell is going on?

Jean-Luc Picard sat on the bridge of the *U.S.S. Enterprise.*

It had taken many years of effort, but he'd finally worked his way up to bridge duty. As a parting gift before taking command of the *U.S.S. Titan,* Riker had granted him the promotion, both to that position and to the rank of lieutenant commander. Picard had taken Riker and Troi's long-ago words to heart and focused himself. He intended to serve Captain Thomas Halloway and his new first officer, Commander Data, to the best of his ability.

"Analysis," Halloway said from the command chair.

From the tactical station, Security Chief Christine Vale reported, "We've got a bunch of *Sovereign*-class ships—or at least ones that match the hull configuration—and a lot of them have a registry of NCC-1701-E. No good readings on whatever it is that is at the center of all this."

"Neat trick," Halloway muttered.

Picard spoke up. "Captain, I believe I know what is happening. It is a quantum fissure, and they are *Enterprises* from different quantum realities."

Data whirled around in his chair, and Picard again found himself feeling a pang of regret. The android was dressed in a red-trimmed uniform, the one he would've worn had he not died in the battle against Shinzon.

Picard knew what was going on. Just as Q had sent him to inhabit himself in three different time frames almost a decade ago, Q had sent Picard to inhabit himself in each of these *Enterprises*, except his own.

"An intriguing hypothesis, Mister Picard," Data said.

"It's not a hypothesis, Commander, it's fact—and what's more, I can prove it. With your permission?"

Data nodded.

Picard put the sensor data he'd just accumulated on the main viewer, showing that each of the ships they were sharing this space with had a different quantum signature.

Halloway stroked his Vandyke beard. "Data—is that even *possible*?"

"Theoretically, yes. I believe Mister Picard is correct that we have encountered a quantum fissure."

Halloway ordered, "Lieutenant Vale, try to hail the other ships—see if anyone answers."

"Yes, si—" Something caught Vale's attention on her tactical status board. "Captain, one of the ships is charging weapons!"

Jean-Luc Picard sat on the bridge of the I.K.S. Qu'.

The heavy chains weighed him down, chafing his neck and wrists and ankles, preventing him from moving without the edges of the shackles cutting into his skin. Every time the wounds scabbed over, one of the Klingons made sure to rip the scabs open so they could be sliced through anew, never quite healing.

He was seated at the feet of the command chair. Once, that chair had been his. Indeed, he'd held on to it longer than most of his fellow UESPA captains. Eventually, he had been conquered, taken by the Klingons, whose empire now spanned most of the Alpha and Beta quadrants, and with the conquest of Bajor almost complete, they would likely take on the Gamma Quadrant next.

Picard had destroyed the ship that went after Enterprise, a defiant gesture he'd accomplished even as the boarding parties were rounding up his crew. They were all dead now, executed in front of him: Riker's throat cut, Data deactivated and disassembled, La Forge disemboweled, Yar shot while trying to escape, Crusher and Troi both violated and strangled, Argyle decapitated. . . .

Because the Klingon ship was destroyed, the fleet general took *Enterprise,* rechristened her, and claimed her as his own.

The doors to the bridge opened, and the heavy tread of Klingon boots heralded the conqueror's arrival.

His cassock billowing behind him as he moved to the center seat, General Worf, son of Mogh, bellowed, "Report! What has happened?"

The Klingon who had taken over Yar's tactical station said, "I do not know, my lord. We are surrounded by ships of similar design to that of the *Qu'.*"

"Impossible." Worf kicked Picard in the ribs as he sat down. The former captain winced but made no outward showing, knowing that the Klingon would reward that with another kick. "All the Federation ships of this class were destroyed."

"I cannot explain it, my lord."

"I can," Picard found himself saying.

Worf looked down. He grabbed the chain attached to the shackle around Picard's neck and yanked him forward. Picard couldn't help wincing as the sides of the shackles bit into his chin. "Explain yourself, slave."

The pull of the shackle made it hard to breathe, but Picard managed to say, "We have entered a different universe. If you scan the other vessels for their quantum signature, you will find that they're all different."

The Klingon at tactical said, "The slave is lying! All matter in the universe has the same quantum signature!"

Worf let go of Picard. He tried to adjust the neck shackle to a more comfortable position as he lay on the deck.

Worf rose. "Of course he is lying. This is a Federation trick."

"There is no Federation, thanks to you!" Picard cried. "I'm telling you the truth, you're just too blind to see it!"

"It does not matter." Worf smiled viciously. "Target the nearest ship and fire."

Picard sat helpless, powerless to do anything about it.

18

—◆—

Enterprise
Quantum fissure, Gorsach system

The end of the universe

"ON SCREEN," WORF SAID.

Leybenzon centered the view on the ship that was firing on them, saying, "That is the ship I could not identify the registry of, sir."

Worf didn't find that too surprising, all things considered.

The ship fired, scoring a direct hit.

"Shields down to forty percent," Leybenzon said. "No damage. They outgun us."

"Hail them, Lieutenant. Tell them to stand down or we will return fire."

"Several vessels are hailing us," Leybenzon said. Worf looked up to see the tactical officer struggling with the comm traffic. "Sir, I believe one of them is the ship that fired on us."

"On screen."

"It's audio only, sir."

"Very well."

Then Worf heard the sound of his own voice. *"This is General Worf of the* Imperial Klingon Ship Qu'. *I claim all these ships for the glory of the Klingon Empire!"*

Everyone on the bridge looked at Worf. He ordered, "Lieutenant Leybenzon, open fire on the *Qu'*, all phasers and quantum torpedoes."

"Aye, sir." Leybenzon sounded gratified.

The Klingon thought he was, in essence, firing on himself.

Worf got up and then ordered, "All weapons, fire at your discretion, Lieutenant."

"Yes, *sir*," Leybenzon said.

Worf walked over to ops. "Kadohata, I need you to work with Commander La Forge and prepare a broad-spectrum warp field."

From the engineering station, La Forge asked, "Captain, are you sure that's a good idea?"

"A broad-spectrum warp field *will* collapse the fissure."

"Perhaps, but . . . are you sure collapsing it's a good idea?"

Leybenzon reported, "Direct hit to *Qu'* on its starboard bow. Their shields are down to fifty percent—but ours are now at twenty percent. Minor damage to secondary hull."

Worf knew that this was the proper course of action. What was happening *now* was exactly what had happened to him nine years ago, and so the solution *had* to be the same.

Suddenly, Worf found himself wondering. Q was involved, which meant that the rules were different. *What if Q has manipulated events deliberately in order to force me to do precisely this—and further whatever mad plan he is engaged in?*

Second-guessing Q was a fool's game, and Worf did not consider himself a fool. His advice to Picard yesterday was still sound: ignore Q.

"I am sure," he said to La Forge. "Prepare the field."

"All right," La Forge said, moving back to the engineering console, "but we can't engage the field while we're under fire."

Worf nodded grimly. "Understood."

On the *F.S.S. Enterprise,* Lieutenant Lio Battaglia said from the tactical console, "One of the ships is engaging another one."

Data stood up from the first officer's position and moved to stand next to Lieutenant Commander La Forge at ops. "Geordi, scan the subatomic matter in the surrounding space for its quantum signature and then match it to the *Enterprise*s around us."

Nodding, La Forge moved his fingers across the

console even as he said, "I get you—you're hoping to find the right one."

"Correct."

Picard nodded, thinking that this was the key to finding his *Enterprise*.

"Uh-oh." La Forge looked up at Data. "The ship that's being fired on is the one that's from these parts, Data."

Picard ordered Sara Nave at conn, "Full impulse, Lieutenant! Put us between the two ships!"

"Aye, sir. Full impulse." To her credit, she didn't hesitate, immediately moving the *Enterprise* into the line of fire.

On the *U.S.S. Enterprise,* Picard turned to Miranda Kadohata at the ops station. "Commander, scan for the quantum signatures of the ships around us— and also of the subatomic matter in space."

Commander Madden asked, "Sir? Why that?"

"If I'm right, Number One"—*and thanks to Data, I know I am,* Picard thought—"we've gone into a different universe."

Kadohata reported, "You're right, sir. Each ship has a different quantum signature."

"Many of them are the same," Hedril said. "I'm picking up a lot of thought patterns that are . . . familiar. But different." She shook her head, almost as if coming out of a daze. "It's very disorienting, Captain."

Picard put a comforting hand on the Cairn counselor's arm, then turned to Kadohata. "Find the *Enterprise* that matches that of the subatomic matter."

From behind him at tactical, Worf said, "Captain, one of the ships is firing! The vessel's identification indicates that it is Klingon, sir."

Urgently, Kadohata added, "Sir, they're firing on the ship that's local to this universe!"

Picard ordered, "Full impulse, Perim! Put us between the two ships!"

"Aye, sir, full impulse." The *Enterprise* moved into the line of fire.

On the *U.S.S. Enterprise,* Christine Vale said from the tactical station, "Sir, that *Enterprise* is taking a pounding. Two of the other *Enterprise*s are moving in to assist." Picard noted that Vale's tone was such that she expected their *Enterprise* to do the same. In the meantime, he was running some scans of his own, based on what he remembered from a nine-year-old log report by Worf.

Thomas Halloway and Data were flanking Vale at tactical. The captain shook his head. "We're not getting involved in local territorial disputes, Lieutenant."

"Captain," Data said, "I do not believe this dispute is 'local.' Based on Lieutenant Commander Picard's analysis, none of these vessels are native to the same universe."

"Excuse me, sir," Picard said, his analysis complete, "but one of them is."

Halloway turned an unkind gaze on Picard. The captain didn't appreciate junior officers interrupting the senior staff.

Undaunted, Picard continued. "Sir, I believe the best way to collapse the fissure and return us all to our proper places is to use a broad-spectrum warp field."

Data considered. "That course of action stands an excellent chance of success."

"Yes," Picard said urgently, "but only if the *Enterprise* native to this universe does it."

Looking at the captain, Data said, "That would ensure the best chance of success, Captain."

"Find the *Enterprise* that's native, and—" Halloway said.

"We have, sir," Picard said. "It's the one being fired upon."

Vale added, "And their shields are down to twenty percent."

"All right, all right," Halloway said, "but I'd better damn well not have cause to regret this, Mister Picard."

"You won't, sir."

Halloway ordered, "Full impulse, Mister Branson. Put us in the fight."

"Aye, sir, full impulse."

On the *U.S. Enterprise,* Picard turned to his CO. "Captain, I believe the ship being fired on is the one native to this universe—they *must* be saved, as they're the only ones who can close the rift!"

Kadohata turned around. "Sir, with all due respect, we don't know that. Parallel universe theory is just that—we don't have any raw data to support—"

Ignoring the second officer, Picard said to the young man next to him, "Captain—Wes—I *know* that this is true!"

Picard couldn't help it. Even though he saw the face of his commanding officer, all he could see was the young man who walked onto his bridge sixteen years earlier. Here and now, he was Picard's superior, and he had to trust that their bond was strong.

The smile finally grew on Wesley's face. "I've always trusted you before, Jean-Luc. Tasha, raise shields, ready phasers and photon torpedoes."

From the tactical station, Lieutenant Commander Tasha Yar said, "Aye, sir."

"Full impulse, Laren. Put us between the two ships."

On the *I.S.S. Enterprise,* Picard dared not join the battle. There was nothing to be gained, and a scientific explanation of the need to preserve this universe's *Enterprise* would fall on deaf ears—and likely give Lore the excuse he needed to ascend to the captaincy via assassination.

On the *I.K.S. Qu',* Picard tried to urge General Worf to stop the attack, but his pleas were met with several boot heels to his head. When the other *Enter-*

*prise*s moved in to defend, Worf laughed contemptu-
ously and said they would all die at his hands.

On the *U.S.V. Enterprise,* Picard instructed the ship
to move, to raise shields, and to arm weapons.

"Commander, look," Kadohata said.

Worf saw that Kadohata had changed the view to
a wider field, and several of the other ships—if
they truly were *Enterprises*—were taking up aggressive positions to the *Qu'.*

"Sir," Leybenzon said, "you'll want to hear this."

Nodding, Worf said, "Proceed."

A cacophony sounded over the speakers.

"This is Captain Jean-Luc Picard of the U.S.S.
Enterprise, *ordering you to stand down."*

"This is Captain Jean-Luc Picard of the F.S.S.
Enterprise, *ordering you to stand down."*

"This is Captain Wesley Crusher of the U.S.
Enterprise, *ordering you to stand down or we will
open fire."*

"This is Captain Thomas Halloway of the U.S.S.
Enterprise—"

"This is Captain William T. Riker of the Starship
Enterprise—"

"This is Captain Data of the E.S.S. Enterprise—"

"This is Captain Jean-Luc Picard of the U.S.S.
Stargazer—"

"This is Captain Jean-Luc Picard of the U.S.S. Sovereign—"

A few others came in languages that the universal translator apparently could not handle. One was in a very old Klingon dialect Worf was able to translate as the captain identifying himself as "Worf Rozhenko of the *U.S.S. Enterprise.*"

"Several of the *Enterprises* are opening fire on the *Qu',*" Leybenzon said.

Worf ordered, "Engage the warp field."

"Some of the systems were damaged—gotta reroute," answered La Forge.

Kadohata said, "Deflectors have power." She ran her fingers over her console. "Done—warp field ready at your discretion."

"Okay," La Forge reported, "full power."

Worf said, "Activate."

"Warp field online," Kadohata said.

The last time, Worf used the warp field from a shuttlecraft to collapse the field, and he knew the stronger broad-spectrum warp field of the *Enterprise* would work even faster.

It was with a rising sense of dread that the Klingon saw the quantum fissure expand.

He stood up.

"The fissure's expanding, sir," Kadohata said.

Worf angrily walked over to the ops console and studied the readings. *It should have worked.*

Damn you, Q.

"Disengage the field."

"We can't. It's locked in, we—" Kadohata looked up. "Sir!"

Worf saw that the fissure's diameter had doubled, its event horizon now nearing some of the *Enterprise*s.

On the *U.S.S. Enterprise,* Captain Halloway said, "Okay, that *can't* be good. Mister Branson, get us the hell out of here, warp one."

Branson shook his head. "Warp drive's not available, sir."

From the science station, Picard felt the ship explode around him as the fissure swallowed the *Enterprise.*

On the *U.S. Enterprise,* Tasha Yar said, "Shields down to ten percent! Another shot, and we're done for!"

"Evasive maneuvers," Captain Crusher ordered. "Laren, get us the hell out of here, warp two!"

"I can't get the engines online!" Ro said.

The ship exploded around Picard as the fissure swallowed the *Enterprise.*

On the *F.S.S. Enterprise,* Picard's first officer said, "Data to engineering. Wesley, the fissure is expanding—we need warp power."

"We don't have it, sir. Best I can give you is half—"

From the captain's chair, Picard watched the ship explode around him as the fissure swallowed the *Enterprise.*

On the *I.K.S. Qu',* most of the bridge crew were dead or injured, the various *Enterprise*s having finally gotten through the mighty vessel's shields. Picard was trapped under a beam that had fallen to the deck, crushing his leg.

General Worf sat in the command chair, angrily pounding it with his fist. "Destroy them! Destroy them all!"

The fissure swallowed the *Qu'.*

On the *Enterprise,* Worf watched, his eyes riveted on the screen, as the fissure expanded. He asked La Forge, "Can we engage the warp drive?"

"It'd be risky."

Worf faced the chief engineer and observed, "We have very little to lose."

"Good point." La Forge manipulated some controls. "Try it now."

Faur tried. "It's not working."

"I was afraid of that." La Forge looked up. "The warp field won't form."

Kadohata asked, "What if—"

Worf watched the ship explode as the fissure swallowed the *Enterprise.*

The last thing Jean-Luc Picard heard before the universe ended was a familiar smarmy voice.

"That's all, folks!"

19

Somewhere . . .

JEAN-LUC PICARD FELT LIKE HE WAS NOWHERE.

This wasn't the all-white "afterlife." He felt himself floating, unfettered by gravity or by much of anything. There was nothing to see, no point of reference to mark his position, no ground to stand on, nothing.

Is this death? he wondered. Just like the last time, when Q had manipulated him to command three different *Enterprises*, he felt himself die more than once. Then, it was to save the galaxy from an anti-time vortex.

This . . . this nothingness Picard felt *had* to be death.

Hadn't it?

If only Picard could stand—or move—or speak—or *do* something.

He couldn't hear, couldn't speak—until suddenly he heard voices from all around him, speaking in gibberish.

"Is [The end] this (Is {Another chance} he?) the [is here.] one? (He is.) Will [At {for salvation} last] he (Is he capable?) speak [it is] {is here} for (He doesn't) this [over.] universe? (seem to {once again.} be much.)"

Picard didn't hear the words as he felt them. He couldn't pinpoint where they were coming from and could barely comprehend them.

He tried to speak but could not.

"Yes," said a familiar voice, "this is the one who destroyed the universe."

At last, Picard found his voice. "Q?" He could not see the trickster—nor could he see whoever was speaking—but that was definitely Q's voice.

"Be quiet, Jean-Luc," said the disembodied voice of Q with surprising gentleness. "You'll have your moment to speak. I have to prepare the ground first."

"What do (I've seen) they [The last one] do with (more impressive) [was much more] those {Not bad.} things sticking out [interesting.] of their (specimens.) bodies?"

"I wouldn't be overly concerned with their rather pathetic physical form. He is a fine representative of humanity, and while they don't seem like much, they have the potential for much more. I realize that, gazing upon Jean-Luc Picard, you see only a weak, fleshy, unimpressive mortal with an unfortunate nose, follicular difficulty, and a tendency to speechify that would put even the most forgiving audience to sleep—"

Picard would have sighed. Q never tired of his put-downs or the sound of his own voice.

"—but he got here. He destroyed the universe. He did it by penetrating the defenses of the Final World. He did it by moving across the space of parallel time lines and reacting instantly to the chaos around him without hesitation or confusion and by making sure that those around him did what was necessary. This, my friends, is a species that only a few short moments ago was so convinced that its homeworld was the center of the universe that they condemned the most learned of them for daring to say otherwise."

"I (So they) rather [This {How did he} is] like {get to the} his nose, (behave [supposed {Final World,} to impress] barbarically.) actually. [us?] {then?}"

"You don't understand—they've progressed from that. And done so at quite the pace. Each setback, each challenge, they adapt and come back stronger— and then make new mistakes, but that's rather the point. They make *new* ones. If you'd asked me two or three moments ago if they would be the ones, I would have laughed in your faces—they were all impressed with their ability to make fire then, and now they have begun the process of comprehending reality, space, and time."

Listening to this, Picard was stunned—especially since, much as it galled him to admit it, most of what he had learned about "reality, space, and time" he had learned from Q, between living his own past and the anti-time test he put them to.

"It's nothing (It's the) we [We're] haven't {It's [bored] dull.} ever seen (same old [with] story.) before. [this!]"

"What are you saying?"

"This (This) [This] {This universe} [universe] (universe) universe {must} must [must] (must die.) die. {die.} [die.]"

"That's it?" Picard found his voice once again.

"Yes. (Yes.) [Yes.] {Yes.} This universe (This universe) [This universe] {This universe will die.} [must die.] (bores us.) is dull."

Jean-Luc Picard couldn't believe it. It wasn't enough that Q had apparently had a *purpose* to all his tormenting of the *Enterprise* crew, and Picard in particular. It wasn't enough that the fate of the universe was tied up in some ridiculous game. But all Picard could do was *float* here while this group of disembodied beings condemned all life as he knew it to cease to be.

He found himself thinking about everything Q ever did, much of which was making sense in light of the past two days. Not all of it. Allowing Data to laugh didn't really have much to do with what was happening—it had been a parting gift from Q, a rare magnanimous gesture.

Except even his selfish gestures appear now to

have meaning. Q chose to send Picard back to when he got his artificial heart. That had appeared to be an excuse to torment Picard. However, it also seemed to be another magnanimous gesture—it allowed Picard to be an alternate version of himself.

It was absurd.

Completely, totally, in all ways absurd.

The first sound that came out of Picard's mouth was a short, "Heh." He felt his lips curl back into a smile.

First, he just chuckled, shaking his head.

That grew into a laugh.

Which grew into a guffaw.

Before he knew it, Picard was having trouble breathing, he was laughing so hard. Life and death all seemed to be a matter of whimsy in any case, so why not indulge in the most whimsical thing he could manage? Certainly this whole exercise was one big joke, so why not go along with it?

He continued to laugh and laugh until he could no longer breathe.

"Much [Much] (Much) {Much} [better.] better. {better.} (better.)"

Picard was still laughing when he found himself prone, lying on rock.

The sensation of *being* somewhere was enough of a shock—because it was a contrast to the nothingness he'd just come from. Looking around, Picard saw that he was on the angled floor of the cavern.

There was no sign of Kadohata, Leybenzon, Stolovitzky, or de Lange, but Picard did hear voices up ahead. He recalled that La Forge and Kadohata's X-ray and magnetic scans revealed that the cavern opened up into a large space—one that was apparently full of people, based on the noise.

The captain tapped his combadge. "Picard to *Enterprise.*" True, he'd seen his ship destroyed—along with all the others from the various universes that had come through the fissure—but life and death appeared to be malleable concepts today.

No response. *Of course, if they're still proximate to Gorsach V, they'd be out of the range of the combadge.*

Looking ahead down the incline, Picard thought, *We went to a great deal of trouble to find out what's in here.*

He stood up and walked forward.

20

U.S.S. Titan
Gum Nebula

CAPTAIN WILL RIKER AND COUNSELOR DEANNA
Troi stood at the window of their shared quarters.
The stars stopped streaking and normalized to
points of light. *Titan* had dropped out of warp and
arrived at the Vela 3AG system.

Recalling the premission briefing, *Titan* was supposed to come into the system at an angle that
would provide Will with a view of the star and its
fourth planet and its ten moons from his cabin
port—it was the reason he'd awakened so early, to
catch the vista he was promised.

The captain was rather pleased to see that view
was even more spectacular than promised.

From behind him, Troi said, "It's beautiful."

Grinning, Riker said, "And today, we get to see what makes it tick."

He turned around and kissed his wife. *This is the way to start a day—a new star system to explore, and my* imzadi *to share it with.*

Bravo Station
Sector 221, Alpha Quadrant

Admiral Elizabeth Paula Shelby's persual of Starfleet records was interrupted by a comm from Bravo Station's operations center. *"Ops to Admiral Shelby."*

She tapped her combadge. "Go ahead."

"Admiral, this is Ensign Galeckas. Something's happened to the Inwood.*"*

Shelby sighed. The *Runabout Inwood* had just departed with crew replacements for Shelby's former command, the *Trident.* "Define 'something.'"

"Engine trouble, Admiral. Lieutenant Cintron says that they're experiencing a plasma leak in the nacelles and they need to turn back."

Shelby ordered, "Alert Captain Mueller that her crew replacements are going to be late."

"Aye, aye, Admiral."

Shelby thought about it. "Belay that, Ensign. I'll contact the captain myself." Kat Mueller had been Shelby's first before her promotion, and this would be a perfect excuse to check on her old command.

"Yes, sir," Galeckas said.

If nothing else, Shelby preferred talking to Mueller than worrying about the Borg.

I.K.S. Gorkon
Klingon Empire

Captain Klag, son of M'Raq prowled the corridors of his ship.

"Bridge to captain."

It was the voice of the second-shift commander. Klag couldn't remember her name. "Speak."

"Sir, we have detected a warp trail that matches that of the Kinshaya ship, and it leads to the Trakliv system. We have changed course to intercept and will arrive in one hour."

"Good. I will be on the bridge shortly."

Even as the bridge door rumbled aside letting Klag in, the operations officer reported, "Sir, picking up the Kinshaya ship!"

The words had been directed at the second-shift commander; therefore, the young officer was shocked when Klag asked, "How far is it, Ensign?"

Whirling around, the ensign composed himself. "Sir, they are in orbit of Trakliv VII."

The pilot said, "Confirmed. We can intercept them in ten minutes."

"On screen." Klag walked to the front of the bridge. The forward viewer showed the Kinshaya ship in a polar orbit of the system's seventh planet. "Pilot, bring us to an intercept course. Gunner, arm all weapons and raise shields." Klag smiled. "It is a good day to die!"

Imperial *Warbird Valdore*
Romulan Star Empire

"We have nothing to say to you, traitress," Subcommander Norvid crowed.

Commander Donatra leaned forward in her chair. "I'm not the traitress, Norvid, Horrhae was for firing on an Imperial warbird. She has paid for that mistake with her life—don't make the same mistake. Three more *Mogai*-class vessels will arrive shortly. If you survive the encounter, you will be brought up on charges and executed very publicly."

"Our orders came from the praetor." Norvid sounded hesitant.

"Indeed? How do you know this? Did you see the order? Do you truly imagine that any praetor worth her salt would order you to fire on a loyal soldier of the empire?"

"You supported the usurper."

"So did the praetor. We were all fooled by that Reman trickster, but he has paid. You command this fleet now, Norvid. Will you lead them to victory or disgrace?"

There was a lengthy pause.

Liravek reported, "All three birds-of-prey are standing down weapons, Commander."

Thank the Elements, Donatra thought, relieved. "You've made the right choice, Norvid."

"I've made no choice yet, Commander. You are bound for Artalierh?"

That fact was not well-known but had obviously been transmitted by a spy on *Valdore*. "That is our destination."

"Our communications systems are not strong enough for real-time communication with the Two Worlds from here, but Artalierh has communication amplifiers and relays that allow such. We will escort you there and determine the source of the commander's orders."

And what happens when the truth of the orders comes out? Donatra wondered. Even if Tal'Aura or one of her lackeys had been responsible, Donatra's surviving the attack would lead her to deny the orders, especially with the convenient scapegoat of the deceased Commander Horrhae. *If she does deny it, I suspect I can then count on Norvid's support.* Donatra smiled. Every little bit helped.

"Agreed, Subcommander. We will proceed as soon as *my* other vessels arrive." Donatra made sure to emphasize the possessive pronoun. These were vessels whose commanders had sworn fealty to Donatra. It didn't hurt to remind Norvid of that fact.

The remainder of the fleet arrived, and all the ships proceeded to Artalierh without incident.

• • •

Karemma trading vessel *Shakikein*
Gamma Quadrant

DaiMon Neek stared angrily at Vogusta over the viewer. For over a year, the Ferengi had been asking the Karemma merchant about Leyles ink. He had been insistent that he would pay "any price" to obtain some of the ink.

Finally, he broke into a pointy-toothed grin. *"Sometimes I'm reminded why I like doing business with you, Vogusta. Your honesty is very refreshing."*

"If you say so," Vogusta said with a sigh. "So we have a deal?"

"Three boxes of Leyles ink for one of the cases of kanar."

"Three boxes for all three cases, DaiMon, or I take my business elsewhere. I'm sure if I have Shipmaster Darsook take us through the anomaly, I can find any number of sources of *kanar* at more reasonable prices *and* someone who'd be willing to take the ink off my ha—"

"Fine, fine," Neek said quickly, *"one box per case of* kanar." He smiled. *"I'll see you in the morning, Vogusta."*

The wall shimmered as Neek's face faded from view. Vogusta returned to his hammock and continued reading until he fell asleep.

He was awakened by the voice of Operator Zali saying, *"Vogusta, this is the flight deck. Please respond."*

Blinking himself awake, Vogusta got out of the hammock. Noting the time on the display unit near the hammock, he realized that they were probably arriving at Gaia. He placed his hand on the intercom control. "This is Vogusta."

"Sir, Shipmaster Darsook has requested that I inform you that we've arrived and the transfer of goods is proceeding, and DaiMon Neek sends his regards."

"Excellent," Vogusta said. "Is my presence required?"

"No, sir."

"Thank you. Out." Vogusta went back to sleep, pleased that another successful transaction had taken place.

Malon *Supertanker Keta*
Delta Quadrant

Controller Sheel turned to Refeek at the flight control console against the bridge's starboard bulkhead. "Increase to maximum."

Refeek whirled around and squinted at him. "Controller, we're *at* maximum."

Glowering at the young man, Sheel said, "No, we're at our maximum safe *cruising* speed. I want us to go to our *emergency* speed."

"Sir," Refeek said, casting a furtive glance at Liswan, "regulations say that we can go to emergency speed only in . . . well, an emergency."

Sheel let out a long breath. "Refeek, one of our shields is about to collapse."

"Well, we have three of them, don't we?" Refeek asked. "I mean, don't we have three so that if one fails the other two will keep going?"

"No, we have three because we don't have enough power to run four. How many instances of shield failure have there been where the other shields didn't immediately collapse in a cascade effect?"

His voice very small now, Refeek said, "Three, maybe?"

"It's a trick question, Refeek—the answer is none. As soon as that shield goes down, it'll be a matter of seconds before the others go with it. In fact, it could happen at any second, and I'd hate to think that we all died of theta radiation poisoning because of the precious time we lost because you were asking *stupid questions!*"

Refeek actually flinched at the last two words, before turning around and working his console.

"Uh, sir," Liswan said quickly, "that may not be such a good idea. The shields may not be able to tolerate—"

"Liswan, is there any chance that we'll make it to KMH-5 at our current speed before the shield collapses?"

"Well, no," Liswan said. "Remlap said it'd be—"

"—twelve hours at the most. If we increase speed, there's a chance we'll make it to KMH-5 before the shield collapses. If we *don't* increase speed, there's *no* chance we'll make it. I don't know about you, but I know which option I prefer."

Nodding, Liswan said, "I withdraw my objection, Controller."

Dryly, Sheel said, "Very generous of you. Now if you'd be so kind as to go down to Remlap and see if she can keep our shields intact long enough to get there."

"Of course." Liswan quickly left the bridge.

To Sheel's relief, Remlap was able to hold the shields together, and the *Keta*'s waste was dumped into KMH-5 without difficulty. Sheel ordered the shields to be taken off-line. He tried not to think about what it was going to cost to repair them. . . .

21

———

Gorsach IX

After the end of the universe

PICARD WALKED FORWARD, THE STONE WALLS
around him widening. Then, suddenly, there was
light, and the noise of cheering crowds was like a
wall of sound.

The chamber was wide but not deep. A pathway
bisected the room, surrounded on both sides by
bleacher-style seats. Those seats faced a wall made
up of metal gratings, with a red flag in the center
emblazoned with a black representation of a falcon.
In front of the flag was a small raised circular stage
that faced the seats.

The audience was human, most a literal version

of the "great unwashed." Ordinary citizens who lived in abject poverty, without access to proper bathing facilities or a regular change of clothes— some barely with access to food—who came to these show trials not out of any sense of civic duty but because it was a source of entertainment in a life that had been made empty by oppression.

Pacing in front of the bleachers were four uniformed soldiers wearing full-body suits that were interwoven with circuitry enhancing their performance, as well as the ability to dispense drugs to engender loyalty. Picard found himself thinking of the Jem'Hadar, the soldiers of the Dominion, who had a dependency on ketracel-white. *Plus ça change, plus c'est la même chose.*

The captain had been here before, or at least somewhere like it. When they first encountered Q, the entity had brought Picard and three of his officers to a place like this, a facsimile of a twenty-first-century third-world court. Where those whose guilt was predetermined were put on trial for purposes that more resembled entertainment than justice. These places had practiced their laughable form of jurisprudence—where guilt was assumed, and justice was a circus.

The crowd jeered at Picard, the guards motioned him forward. He walked up the two stairs to the stage and took a seat in the solitary chair. Picard was brought back here again. The captain thought, Plus ça change, *indeed.*

A tall man wearing an elaborate floor-length

coat, an equally elaborate hat, and carrying a staff as tall as him, stood in the center of the space. Next to him was a diminutive man with a fierce face holding a gong. The shorter man struck the gong twice, followed by the tall man saying, "All present stand and make respectful attention to the honored judge!"

The crowd got to their feet even as a large angled platform came into view from the rear of the room. It hovered several meters above the ground, and a long bar served as a lever, giving the judge who sat in it free movement across the chamber. An elaborate throne sat at the platform's center, two golden lion's-head poles framed the front corners of the platform. Q sat, once again dressed in the elaborate red robes, red gloves, large necklace, and black hat that the judges of these courts wore. With a gesture, Q silenced the crowd and bid them sit.

"Well done, *mon capitaine*," Q said as he floated in over the heads of the crowd. "I thought you'd *never* figure it out."

That prompted jeering from the crowd. Some of the guards stepped forward, and they quieted down, though one or two still chortled and pointed at the stage.

Picard shook his head. "All of it. Farpoint Station, giving Riker the power of the Q, sending us to meet the Borg, sending me back to my Academy days, testing us with the anti-time vortex—even teaching Data to laugh—all of it was part of the preparation?"

Smirking, Q said, "Yes, Jean-Luc, all of it, and more. Sending microbrain through all those parallel universes, for example. That trick he used on the fissure was a necessary catalyst, and he wouldn't have known to do that without that little jaunt I sent him on."

Picard stared at Q in shock. In truth, at this point, nothing Q did really could surprise him. "You did that?"

"Of course."

"Why?"

The crowd laughed at that, and one or two of them threw small items toward the stage. They missed Picard, and he ignored them. A guard stepped forward and pointed his weapon at the instigators.

Testily, Q said, "Oh, enough of this." He waved his arm, and everything vanished in a blinding flash of light, leaving Picard and Q alone in the courtroom. "Much better. They're good local color, but the noise does get to one after a while."

"I asked a question, Q."

"Yes, you asked why. An odd question for you to ask, Jean-Luc, given what was at stake—and what was accomplished. You see, the fate of the entire universe hung in the balance—*all* of it."

At last, Picard put it together. "Those . . . those beings—who were they?"

"I'm afraid They cannot be named as such, Jean-Luc. We've tried, but They are above such things."

"Including the Q?"

Clapping twice with his gloved hands, Q said, "Well done, Jean-Luc. Yes, They are greater even than the Q—and if They had destroyed the universe, the Continuum would've been gone with it."

Nodding in understanding, Picard said, "So you cheated."

Q straightened, offended. "I beg your pardon?"

"You cheated. You prepared us—prepared me, prepared Worf—manipulating us to save your own skin."

"And yours," Q said archly. "And microbrain's, and Randy's, and your dear Beverly's, and La Forge's, and newt-boy's . . ." He smirked. "Even the Borg's."

Picard considered the mention of the Borg. "But it wasn't a fair test. You lied to Them."

"One cannot lie to Them—and everything I said was the truth. You did master the paradox, which earned you the right to be judged. The rest of it you did yourself."

"The laughter."

Q nodded. "And I must say, Jean-Luc, what most worried me was that the fate of the universe rested in the hands of the stuffiest human being in the history of the galaxy finding out that he has a sense of humor."

Incredulous, Picard said, "*That* is what makes us special? Our accomplishments, our ambition, our drive to improve ourselves, our ability to adapt—none of that matters?"

"Of course it matters, Jean-Luc, don't be ridiculous," Q snapped, maneuvering the platform close to Picard. He whispered, "But it also matters that you can still laugh. Why do you think the best gift I could give Data was the ability, however briefly, to laugh? Why do you think I showed you what your life would've been if you hadn't gotten into that fight with the Nausicaans? When the reality was restored—"

Picard's eyes widened. "I laughed!"

"That's right."

It had never made any sense to Picard. He wondered why he had laughed when he saw the Nausicaan blade protruding through his chest. When Q showed him what his life would have been like if he'd avoided the fight, Picard was so disgusted that he, once again, picked a fight with a Nausicaan. When he saw himself get stabbed, Picard was overjoyed—and laughed.

"And all of it," Picard said slowly, "was in preparation for this day." He sighed. "How absurd." Q was about to speak; Picard held up a hand. "But that would seem to be the point, wouldn't it?"

"You're learning, Jean-Luc." The throne rose higher.

Picard looked around at the empty courtroom. He had hoped never to see this place again. "So it's finally over?"

"Yes, *mon capitaine*."

"Then I'd like to go back to my ship."

Q rolled his eyes. "Of *course* you would."

As Q raised his hand, Picard thought back on all the times Q visited. Were they truly altruistic?

"Q," Picard asked, "what did going into Sherwood Forest and making me play the role of Robin Hood to Vash's Marian have to do with all this?"

Shrugging, Q said, "I just wanted to see you in tights, Jean-Luc."

With that, Q snapped his fingers, and Picard was gone.

EPILOGUE

———◆———

Enterprise

In orbit of Gorsach IX

THE MOST PECULIAR THING WAS THAT GORSACH IX was still there.

Worf sat in the observation lounge, going over the landing party suggestions made by the department heads. The planet may have been a construction of the strange beings that the captain encountered in Q's company, but it was still a new world to explore.

The same could not be said for Gorsach V. The quantum fissure was gone, and so was the gas giant. It hadn't turned into a red dwarf, it hadn't turned into anything, it was just gone. Kadohata had launched another probe—the first one a casualty of the quantum fissure—while the *Enterprise* returned to the constructed world.

To his great irritation, Worf had no idea what happened. The last thing he remembered was being in a battle with multiple *Enterprises*—and then everything was back to normal. The fissure, Gorsach V, and all the ships vanished.

Captain Picard had reappeared on the bridge in a flash of light. He yanked down his uniform jacket and said, "I see no reason not to continue our mission, Number One, and explore the surface of Gorsach IX."

All the years Worf had served under Captain Picard, and yet this human still had the ability to surprise him. He considered what he read in Picard's report about Q and the end of the universe, and decided that with all things Q, the less he thought about it, the more logical Q's actions became.

Worf noted Leybenzon's security requests. Tapping his combadge, he summoned the lieutenant to the observation lounge.

Leybenzon came and stood at attention. "Sir?"

Turning his chair to face Leybenzon, Worf said, "You have doubled your security requests for the Gorsach IX away team. *Two* security guards for every scientist, plus *eight* on rotating shifts at the base camp."

"Yes, sir. I thought it best to be prudent."

"The threat would appear to have passed, Lieutenant."

Leybenzon shot Worf a look. "Because Q says so? I do not think that is a good reason, sir. While I recognize that there is little we can do against Q, I would be derelict in my duty if I did not try to make the away team as safe as possible."

Worf nodded. "Very well—your request is approved."

"Thank you, sir." He turned to leave.

"There is one more thing," Worf said, which caused the lieutenant to stop and stand at attention again.

"Yes, sir?"

"Doctor Crusher has expressed a concern about your inability to report for your physical."

Leybenzon let out a long breath. "Commander, do you remember that quack back home, Doctor Dryanushkina? Always prescribed lemon juice for everything?"

Allowing himself a small smile, Worf said, "I saw him only once, when I was a boy. He refused to see me again after I ate his medical scanner."

That prompted a laugh from Leybenzon. "Oh, I wish I'd seen that. The point is, I do not like doctors."

"That does not excuse you from your duties."

"Of course, Commander, I do know that. I was simply procrastinating. As soon as the mission to Gorsach IX is complete, I will—"

"No," Worf said, "you will report this afternoon at fifteen hundred. Ensign Stolovitzky will replace you on the away team." Before Leybenzon could object, Worf said, "This matter is *not* up for discussion, Lieutenant. Dismissed." Worf started reading the padd again.

Leybenzon stood still for several seconds. "Yes,

sir, of course, sir. I apologize for being derelict in my duties."

Once the doors closed, Worf set the padd down. This time the smile was bigger. He hadn't thought about Doctor Dryanushkina in a very long time.

After indulging himself for a few more seconds, Worf tapped his combadge. "Worf to Crusher."

"Go ahead."

"Lieutenant Leybenzon will report for his physical at fifteen hundred."

"Thank you, Worf. I really didn't want to remove him from duty."

"You are welcome. Worf out."

He picked up the padd and continued to go over the landing party recommendations.

Geordi La Forge walked into the Riding Club and looked around for the biosignature that matched Miranda Kadohata. She was alone. This would be an easier conversation to have one-on-one.

Putting on a pleasant face, La Forge walked over to her table and asked, "This seat taken, Miranda?"

She smiled. "Not at all, Geordi. Please join me. I was sharing lunch with Beverly. She got called to sickbay—Ensign LaMonica apparently tripped over the sofa in her quarters."

La Forge winced. "She's just not having any luck, is she?"

"I told Beverly to pass along my offer to babyproof her cabin like we did for the kids back home."

"Not a bad idea." Before La Forge could continue, Jordan walked over. "I'll have a synthale."

Jordan nodded and asked Kadohata, "Another iced tea?"

"I'm fine," the second officer said. "I've got to be back on the bridge in ten minutes."

"One synthale, coming up." Jordan walked off.

"So," Kadohata asked, "how goes the preparation for the base camp?"

La Forge said, "Ready. Taurik did a systems check to make sure Q's shenanigans didn't do any damage, but we're good to go."

"Bravo. Once Worf sorts out the away teams, we can start exploring this dull ball."

"Is it really that bad?" La Forge asked.

"No, it's worse." She sighed. "I suppose it's possible that we'll turn something up, but a planet arranged to be perfect strikes me as having little scientific interest. We don't have to bother tracing the origins, since we know the planet was built *and* who built it. I think the most fascinating scientific inquiry involves finding out where something *came* from." Kadohata was leaning forward in her chair now, gesturing so emphatically La Forge feared she'd spill her iced tea on him. "Digging around and finding out how it got there. But there's none of that on Gorsach IX—it was all *put* there by those people the captain met. Takes the fun right out, if you ask me." She looked contritely at La Forge. "I'm going on again. I'm sorry."

"No, that's all right." La Forge held up a hand. "I

see your point—but I'm curious as to *how* the place was built. I mean, making an entire planet? Now, *that's* engineering. First thing I thought this morning when I woke up was, 'Today, I get to check out the weird planet!'"

"Thus perfectly outlining the differences between the theoretician and the engineer," Kadohata added.

"Yeah." La Forge paused while Jordan brought over his synthale. "Thanks, Jordan." He took a sip of the beverage, the syntheholic re-creation of an India Pale Ale. Then he said, "Look, Miranda, we need to talk."

Kadohata frowned. "About what?"

"On the bridge, when we were activating the warp field, you jumped in and used the deflector."

"Yes. I know that Data would probably have checked with you, or consulted with you, but that's because Doctor Soong programmed him to be polite." She paused. "Mum always said, 'Speak your mind and let other people worry about whether or not it gets them cheesed off.' Took four years of the Academy to teach me restraint and respect. Those first two years were a nightmare, believe you me. I was constantly questioning my superiors. Almost resulted in expulsion once or twice, to be honest."

"My mother taught me to respect the chain of command."

"That's right, your mother was in Starfleet."

"Yeah, and she'd be pretty—" La Forge hesitated, then broke into a grin. "She'd be pretty cheesed off if she heard me complaining to a superior officer for doing her job."

Kadohata leaned forward, choosing her words carefully. "Geordi, I miss him too. A lot. He was my mentor back in the day. Data was integral to this crew. It would've been easier if he were here, but he's not."

Shaking his head, La Forge said, "I'm the one who's being a jackass here, and I'm really sorry."

"I've got my own issues."

"Really?" That surprised La Forge.

Kadohata hesitated. "The vision I had was me back home on Cestus. I was a professor at Bacco University, just like Vicenzo. And it was completely *wrong*. That isn't me." She shook her head. "The hell of it is, I haven't called home since then."

Speaking slowly, La Forge asked, "Miranda, how long have you two been married?"

"Seven years next month."

"You really think he's going to think less of you because you feel you belong in Starfleet?"

"You're right." Kadohata went to sip her iced tea and saw the glass was empty. "I suppose this whole thing has me wound up wrong."

"Maybe it does." He put a hand on hers. "Look, Miranda, I've got no experience as a counselor, and my love life could charitably be called a disaster area, so maybe I'm not the best guy to give you advice."

She smiled. "So noted. Carry on."

"Call Vicenzo, trust him."

Nodding, Kadohata said, "You're right. Thank you, Geordi." She added, "I know we've got some work to do on the second-officer-and-chief-engineer dynamic, but I hope I can consider you a friend."

"Definitely."

Kadohata stood up. "I've got to get to the bridge. Cheers." She gave La Forge a wide smile and then added, "Geordi?"

"Yeah?"

"My quarters, tomorrow night, twenty-one hundred—bring the cards, I'll provide the chips."

Frowning, La Forge said, "I beg your pardon?"

"I'm inviting Worf, Beverly, T'Lana, and the captain. Poker. Dealer calls the game, but I swear if anyone calls one of those silly wild-card variants I will taunt them mercilessly."

"Fair enough. What about Leybenzon? He seems like the kind of guy who'd enjoy it."

After considering it for a second, Kadohata nodded. "All right, I'll ask him." She moved toward the exit. "Take care, Geordi."

La Forge drank the last of his ale. He hadn't told Miranda the truth. His first thought waking up this morning was, *Today, Data and I get to check out the weird planet!*

La Forge exited the Riding Club. He wanted to check Taurik's final report on the base camp equipment one more time. *I still miss you, Data.* La Forge smiled, recalling the number of times they had taken all of Data's chips. He started considering who'd be as gullible and readable as Data had been . . . had been. *That was a first.* Maybe that was all he needed—a good, swift reality check.

However, he was at least a little cheered by the fact that he'd be playing a poker game afterward. La Forge had assumed that, with Riker's departure, the weekly poker games would cease, and he found that he was grateful to Kadohata for starting them up again.

T'Lana sat opposite Captain Picard in his ready room, having declined his offer of tea. They had been discussing the crew's reactions to the encounter with Q.

"One more thing, Counselor. How's Commander Kadohata handling her new position?"

"There are the usual difficulties. She is replacing a beloved officer who held the same post."

Picard considered the mixed blessing of Vulcan bluntness. "Do you think these difficulties are ones she can overcome?"

"Yes, sir."

"Is there anything else?"

T'Lana hesitated. "Leading the landing party was unwise."

After taking a sip of his tea, Picard carefully pointed out, "It has been my experience, where Q is concerned, that traditional methods are not applicable."

"I wonder, sir, how often you will be able to find the rationale to go against standard procedure."

The counselor had spoken openly as the captain had requested. Jean-Luc Picard smiled at her. "I appreciate your candor, Counselor, and hope it will continue."

"What concerns me, Captain, is what you will do with that candor."

"Thank you, Counselor. Dismissed."

With that, T'Lana rose, bowed her head slightly to the captain, and left the ready room.

"Deal me out," La Forge said as he rose from the table in Kadohata's quarters. "I need to get something from my cabin."

Kadohata smiled as she shuffled the deck. "If it's a pair of aces to shove up your sleeve, make sure they aren't both diamonds." She stared at the small pile of chips in front of La Forge's seat. *Geordi's not having a good night of it.*

Chuckling, La Forge left, leaving only Picard, T'Lana, and Crusher at the table.

"Did you invite Lieutenant Leybenzon?" T'Lana asked.

"I did. He declined. At first I thought he was just being himself, but he said he's never played the game."

Smirking, Crusher said, "Seems to me like that's the ideal new player."

Kadohata laughed as she put the deck in front of T'Lana, who cut it. "That's what I said. But he also said that he would be more than happy to take any comers in Go."

Picard nodded. "Go is an excellent method for training the strategic mind."

Kadohata started dealing the cards. "Five-card draw, jacks or better to open."

As she took her cards, Crusher said, "Zelik Leybenzon was the most nightmarish physical I've ever given. He complained about every single thing I did, asked the reason behind each test."

Kadohata saw that she had a pair of twos—diamonds and clubs—and three, four, and six, all clubs. "Can anyone open?"

Picard threw in two silver chips.

Crusher did likewise. T'Lana shook her head, folded. Kadohata also tossed in two silver chips.

The captain took three cards, and Crusher took two. Kadohata looked at hers, decided the reward was worth the risk. She took one. She got a five of clubs, a straight flush. Only a higher straight flush could beat her, and that seemed unlikely.

"Check," Picard said.

Crusher put in one gold chip and three silver chips.

Kadohata hoped she was hiding all her "tells." If Crusher was going to bet aggressively, more for her. Kadohata raised the bet, but only by one silver chip.

Smiling, Picard said, "I think not," and folded.

Looking at Kadohata, Crusher said, "You know what I think, Miranda? I think you were pulling for an inside straight, didn't get it, and you're staying in out of pride."

"It'll cost you another silver chip to find that out."

"If you think you can bluff me, forget it; I've played with William Riker." Crusher tossed in a silver chip, then added three gold chips.

Kadohata pretended to study her cards, but this hand was over. The doctor obviously had a good hand, but no way it could beat her straight flush.

La Forge walked back in, holding something in his hand that Kadohata couldn't see.

Kadohata called the bet tentatively, putting in three gold chips. She'd been tempted to raise.

Grinning, Crusher said, "Even if you pulled the straight, it doesn't matter." She laid down four sevens.

"Actually," Kadohata said, putting down her cards, "it's a straight *flush*."

"That's it, I need a new workout partner," Beverly muttered dolefully.

Grinning as she raked in the chips, Kadohata said, "Win some, lose some, Bev."

La Forge leaned over Miranda and put a visor on her head.

T'Lana asked, "What is the significance of that headpiece?"

Miranda took it off, turning it over in her hands. "It was Data's, wasn't it?"

La Forge nodded. "He wore it to every poker game without fail." Looking at T'Lana, he said, "Not very logical, I admit, but—"

"I disagree," T'Lana said.

Miranda smiled at Geordi and placed the visor back on her head. "What's the game?"

."Seven-card high-low," Crusher said, as she dealt the cards.

The poker game went on into the night. . . .

"Jean-Luc, I'm concerned about Lieutenant Leybenzon."

Picard set his padd on the nightstand. "Because he wouldn't attend the poker game?"

"No." She hesitated.

Jean-Luc took the padd out of her hand. "What is it?"

"Patients like Leybenzon are the ones who die on the table because they refuse to share information."

He stroked her cheek. "There is little you can do. You're a good doctor, you will find a way to gain his trust."

"I suppose. I'm just glad Q is gone."

"Well, with Q . . ."

"Jean-Luc?"

The captain indicated the center of their cabin. Beverly turned, and her jaw fell open.

Floating in the center of their cabin were letters that spelled out the words: DON'T COUNT ON IT, JEAN-LUC. YOU HAVEN'T SEEN THE LAST OF ME YET.

After a moment, the words faded into nothingness.

Turning back to look at Jean-Luc, Beverly said, "It really was too much to hope that this would be the last we'd see of him, wasn't it?"

"Far too much."

FINAL INTERLUDE

The Continuum

IT HAD BEEN VERY DIFFICULT FOR HIM NOT TO gloat.

Oh, it was tempting. After all the hardships, all the dismissals, after kicking him out of the Continuum, after stripping him of his powers, after civil war and procreation, it turned out that he was right all along. It took all his willpower—of which he had very little, for what need did an omnipotent being have for willpower?—not to jump up and down and point and laugh and say, "I told you so!"

All right, so it was a human gesture. What was wrong with those, really? After all, humans did save the universe.

He just hoped Jean-Luc didn't make a big fuss about it. Of course, that was why the *Enterprise* captain was so well suited to the job, as Jean-Luc was unlikely *to* make a fuss about it. That ship of his was always going around saving things, anyhow, so adding the universe to the list probably wasn't all that big a deal for the good captain.

Naturally, he spied on Jean-Luc and the good doctor one last time. He couldn't resist. Human sexual practices had always held a bizarre fascination for him—the same way humans loved to gaze upon traffic accidents. The Q reproduced in a much more orderly manner.

Q was, as Jean-Luc had so eloquently put it, "next of kin to chaos." Where was the fun in order?

However, the Continuum liked order. They liked a living universe even more, but they weren't about to let him gloat, even if he had been right.

At the very least, he had to gloat to the family. After all, Q had been right there with everyone else, doubting him, making fun of him. Worse, she abandoned him and their child, poor little innocent q. Well, all right, he wasn't that innocent—he was a holy terror until Kathy managed to calm him down (another point for the humans).

Q was contrite, though she didn't put up with his gloating for very long. As for q, he was growing into a full-blown Q. He'd be guiding lesser lifeforms in no time.

At one point, q asked him, "Dad, will I ever get to save the universe?"

"Anything's possible, son. The universe, you see, is like a giant tapestry." He smirked, even as the universe suddenly appeared before him and Q and q, in the form of a tapestry, woven out of stars and space and gases and nebulae—"starstuff," as one of the brighter specimens of humanity had called it. "And there are so many threads that we still haven't pulled on yet."

Grinning, q reached out with one hand. "How about this one?"

AFTERWORD

———

I WAS IN MY SOPHOMORE YEAR AT FORDHAM UNI-
versity in New York when *Star Trek: The Next Generation* debuted two decades ago with the two-hour
episode "Encounter at Farpoint." My friends and I—
who had watched the show in reruns since we were
kids, who had seen all four (at the time) movies the
day they opened, who had been playing FASA's *Star
Trek* role-playing game for years, who regularly
traded *Star Trek* novels and comic books—awaited
the release with bated breath.

It was the *Nine O'Clock Movie* on WPIX, Channel 11, in New York, the same station on which
we'd seen those reruns of the original series. I sat,
riveted, curious about the new crew, the new ship,
and the cast of virtual unknowns. I knew LeVar
Burton, of course, from *Roots* and *Reading Rain-
bow* and *One in a Million: The Ron LeFlore Story*,
and I had a vague recollection of Patrick Stewart as
one of the few bright spots in an otherwise-dismal
adaptation of *Dune,* but that was it. I found myself

intrigued by the new characters, and impressed with the actors, new and old—in particular Brent Spiner (who I only later realized was Bob Wheeler on *Night Court*).

However, the person who made the greatest impression on me on that historic night in the fall of 1987 was John de Lancie as Q.

God knows, *Star Trek* had its fair share of higher beings who toyed with humanity, from the Metrons in "Arena" to the Organians in "Errand of Mercy" to the swirly thing in "Day of the Dove" to the Excalbians in "The Savage Curtain," but none of them were as much *fun* as de Lancie's Q. The smarminess, the snideness, the impishness, the humor were all incredibly appealing. Rather than the pompous, ethereal posturing or silent manipulation of the higher beings from the original series, Q was *fun.*

Q kept coming back, of course, as all the entertaining characters do, and even showed up on *TNG*'s two twenty-fourth-century successors, *Deep Space Nine* and *Voyager,* as well as in several novels and comic books. And, just as he was there for TNG's beginning on the small screen, he was there for its end, in 1994's "All Good Things . . ."

Over the last few years, it's been my privilege to write all across the *Star Trek* map. I've penned stories involving all five of the TV shows, as well as several of the prose-only series that have sprung up over the past decade: *New Frontier, Corps of Engineers, I.K.S. Gorkon, The Lost Era,* etc. But one character I hadn't written was Q.

AFTERWORD

That changed when I walked into Pocket Books Executive Editor Margaret Clark's office one afternoon, she handed me the outline and first few chapters of J. M. Dillard's *Resistance,* and said, "How'd you like to write one of the *TNG* anniversary books?"

After I picked my jaw up off the floor, I naturally said yes. Having had the opportunity to set up the *Enterprise*-E's movie voyage in *Star Trek Nemesis* in my novel *A Time for War, A Time for Peace,* I didn't imagine that I'd get the chance to help continue the ship's adventures past that feature film.

It took me no time at all to settle on my antagonist. After all, how could we possibly do the twentieth anniversary without Q?

Margaret deserves a *huge* amount of credit here, both for agreeing to let me do the ultimate Q story, and for her expert story guidance, curbing my excesses, and bringing this book into much greater focus. It's no mean feat trying to pull together all of Q's prior appearances, and Margaret is responsible for whatever success I may have achieved in that regard.

She also allowed me to create two new characters for the *Enterprise* crew. The ever-talented Ms. Dillard had already provided the new ship's counselor to replace Deanna Troi (now off with Captain William T. Riker on the good ship *Titan*). Since we'd lost Data in *Nemesis* and Worf was now first officer, the positions of second officer and security chief needed filling, and I took advantage of the opportunity to give us something we hadn't seen on *Trek* before. In the case of Miranda Kadohata, it's a woman dealing with the immediate aftermath of giving birth, something no *Trek* show has truly dealt with in any depth. With Zelik Leybenzon, I wanted to give us a "mustang," a noncommissioned officer who clawed his way up the ranks.

I hope you like what you've seen, and that you've actually read this far through my self-indulgent ramblings.

Thanks must also go to a variety of other people:

Lucienne Diver, my wonderful agent, about whom I can't say enough kind things.

Paula Block at CBS Consumer Products, who continues to be the best licensing person ever.

All the actors who have portrayed members of the Q Continuum on screen: Corbin Bernsen, Olivia d'Abo, Keegan de Lancie, Gerrit Graham, the magnificent Suzie Plakson, Harve Presnell, Lorna Raver, and, of course, the man himself, John de Lancie.

The other actors who have played the characters in this volume, who provided face and voice for me to work with: LeVar Burton (La Forge), Steven Culp (Madden), Elizabeth Dennehy (Shelby), Michael Dorn (Worf), Kirsten Dunst (Hedril), Alexander Enberg (Taurik), Michelle Forbes (Ro), Jonathan Frakes (Riker), John Hancock (Haden), Norman Lloyd (Galen), Gates McFadden (Beverly Crusher),

Colm Meaney (O'Brien), Dina Meyer (Donatra), Kate Mulgrew (Janeway), Stephanie Niznik (Perim), Michael Owen (Branson), Tim Russ (Tuvok), Marina Sirtis (Troi), Brent Spiner (Data, Lore), Patrick Stewart (Picard), Brian Thompson (Klag), and Wil Wheaton (Wesley Crusher).

Several writers who have penned episodes, movies, books, and/or short stories that were of use in the composition of this volume: Ira Steven Behr and Randee Russell (*TNG*'s "Qpid"); Christopher L. Bennett (the novel *Orion's Hounds*); Rick Berman, Brent Spiner, and John Logan (the movie *Star Trek Nemesis*); Kenneth Biller (*Voyager*'s "The Q and the Grey" and "Q2"); Brannon Braga (*TNG*'s "Parallels" and "All Good Things . . ."); Greg Cox (the *Q-Continuum* novel trilogy); Richard Danus (*TNG*'s "Déjà Q"); Peter David (the novels *Q-in-Law; Q-Squared; I, Q; Requiem; After the Fall; Missing in Action;* and *Before Dishonor*); John de Lancie (the novel *I, Q*); J. M. Dillard (the *Star Trek Nemesis* novelization, the novel *Resistance*); Robert J. Doherty (*Voyager*'s "Q2"); René Echevarria (*TNG*'s "True Q"); D. C. Fontana (*TNG*'s "Encounter at Farpoint"); Michael Jan Friedman (the *All Good Things . . .* novelization, the book *Q's Guide to the Continuum,* and the novel *Death in Winter*); David Gerrold (the *Encounter at Farpoint* novelization); Christie Golden (the novella "Into the Queue" in *Gateways: What Lay Beyond*); Robert Greenberger (the book *Q's Guide to the Continuum,* and the novels *A Time to Love* and *A*

Time to Hate); Maurice Hurley (*TNG*'s "Hide and Q" and "Q Who"); Heather Jarman (the novel *String Theory: Evolution*); David Mack (the novels *A Time to Kill* and *A Time to Heal*); Andy Mangels and Michael A. Martin (the novels *Taking Wing* and *The Red King*); Ronald D. Moore (*TNG*'s "Tapestry" and "All Good Things . . ."); Terri Osborne (the short story "'Q'uandary" in *No Limits*); Michael Piller (*Voyager*'s "Death Wish"); Shawn Piller (*Voyager*'s "Death Wish" and "The Q and the Grey"); Gene Roddenberry (*TNG*'s "Encounter at Farpoint" and "Hide and Q"); Hannah Louise Shearer and Robert Hewitt Wolfe (*DS9*'s "Q-Less"); John Vornholt (the novels *A Time to Be Born* and *A Time to Die*); and Dayton Ward and Kevin Dilmore (the novels *A Time to Sow* and *A Time to Harvest*). I also made use of my own material from *Diplomatic Implausibility; Demons of Air and Darkness; The Brave and the Bold; A Time for War, A Time for Peace; Articles of the Federation;* and the *I.K.S. Gorkon* series. The aforementioned Terri Osborne also deserves thanks for coming up with the title for this book, thus providing me with my shortest book title to date. Fitting, since my previous *TNG* book had my longest title. . . .

Various reference sources: *The Star Trek Encyclopedia* by Michael and Denise Okuda, with Debbie Mirek; *Star Charts* by Geoffrey Mandel; Larry Nemecek's *Star Trek: The Next Generation Companion;* and the fantastic (and ever-growing) websites Memory Alpha (www.memory-alpha.org) and the Non-Canon *Star Trek* Wiki (startrek.wikia.com). Also thanks to Infinite Viking for anecdotal assistance, and www.panchobarnes.com for info on the original Happy Bottom Riding Club.

The usual gangs of idiots: my glorious writers group, CGAG; the Forebearance, in particular The Mom; the other folks at Pocket, Marco Palmieri, Ed Schlesinger, Jen Heddle, and Jaime Cerota; my fellow band members in the Boogie Knights (www.boogie-knights.org), for giving me a much-needed musical outlet; the folks at the café, who provided me with an endless supply of iced coffee and bagels while I worked; and the various folks on the assorted *Star Trek* Literature bulletin boards on the internet: the Trek BBS (www.trekbbs.com), Psi Phi (www.psiphi.org), Book Trek (www.booktrek.tk), and, of course, Pocket Books' own board (www.startrekbooks.com) and the official *Star Trek* site (www.startrek.com).

Finally, them that live with me, both human and feline, who provide me with joy and wonderfulness.

It's been twenty years. Ironically, it was on the occasion of *Star Trek*'s twentieth anniversary that Paramount announced it would be launching a new TV show, *Star Trek: The Next Generation*, the following year. Now, twenty years after that show, the franchise continues to plug away. *TNG* spawned three spinoffs, and the number of movies has more than doubled. It's been a fantastic journey, and I'm grateful for the opportunity to help celebrate it.

So here's to twenty more years. And twenty years after that. And so on.

—Keith R.A. DeCandido
somewhere in New York City

STAR TREK

THE NEXT GENERATION®

BEFORE DISHONOR

Peter David

Available November 2007

1

———

The *Einstein*

KATHRYN JANEWAY NEEDED TO SEE IT FOR HERSELF.
She had read the detailed reports provided her
by Seven of Nine. She had spoken at length with
Captain Jean-Luc Picard, about whom she was still
seething. In short, she had all the information she
really required. Going to the Borg cube wasn't
going to accomplish a damned thing.

Yet here she was, on her way, just the same.

Although she was entitled, by her rank of vice-
admiral, to commandeer an entire starship for the
purpose of essaying the trip, she had opted not to
do so. She considered it a waste of resources. Instead she had been content to catch a ride on the
Einstein, a standard science-exploration vessel. The
commander of the *Einstein,* Howard Rappaport,
had been enthused to welcome Janeway aboard.
Short, stocky, but with eyes that displayed a pierc-
ing intellect, Rappaport had peppered her with

questions about all the races that she had encountered during the *Voyager*'s odyssey from the Delta quadrant. It hadn't been something that she'd been overly interested in discussing, but turning down Rappaport's incessant interrogation would have felt like kicking an eager puppy, and so she had accommodated him during their trip as often as she had felt reasonable.

At least she knew he was paying attention, because not only did he hang on every word she spoke, but he kept asking intelligent follow-up questions. Still, at one point he said eagerly, "I wish I'd been there."

Upon hearing that, Janeway had promptly shut him down with a curt "No. You really don't." When she said that, he looked as if he wanted to ask more about her attitude in that regard, but wisely opted to back off when he saw the slightly haunted look in Janeway's eyes.

There were three other Starfleet officers traveling on the *Einstein* with Janeway, all of them purported experts on the Borg. The officers—Commanders Andy Brevoort and Tom Schmidt, and Lieutenant Commander Mark Wacker—were experienced xenobiologists who had been given a simple mandate by Starfleet: Find a way to develop an absolute protection against the Borg should they launch another attack. The general feeling of the United Federation of Planets Council and Starfleet in particular was that, even though they had managed to dodge destruction at the hands of the Borg each and every time, they owed a measure of that success to sheer luck.

The plan was to try to remove luck from the equation and replace it with a practical, proven solution.

The *Einstein* was long on durability but short on amenities. It was designed to cater to scientists, not to top brass or ambassadors or any of that ilk. Janeway's quarters were consequently the most luxurious the ship had to offer yet still quite spare. The admiral didn't care. She didn't tend to stand on ceremony in such matters. Give her breathable atmosphere, functioning gravity, and a steady source of coffee, and Janeway was content.

The admiral was worried she was becoming an addict. The last time she'd been on a starship, she'd studied the warp core too long and decided that it looked like a gigantic antique coffee maker. She'd sworn—at that point—to give up the hideously addictive brew. Yet here she was now, nursing a cup of black coffee while she read over yet again the reports from all the various sources about the monstrous Borg cube that the *Enterprise* had managed to take down pretty much single-handedly. There was a transcript of all of Picard's log entries on the subject, as well as the entries from other crew members, including, most notably, the Vulcan counselor, T'Lana. Janeway shook her head as she read it all, still bristling at the very thought of all that had transpired contrary to her orders.

"How could you, Picard?" she asked rhetorically of the empty room. "How could you put me in that kind of position, just on a hunch?"

"It's what I would have done."

The voice caught her by surprise, because she

had naturally thought she was alone. She turned and, uncharacteristically but understandably, let out a startled yelp.

James T. Kirk was standing in her quarters.

"*What the hell—?!*" Janeway was on her feet, gaping.

Kirk was wearing a very old-style Starfleet uniform, a simple yellow shirt with black collar. He smoothed it down and gave her a wry smile. "Hello, Admiral. Or Kathryn, perhaps? Would it be too forward if I addressed you as Kathryn? Feel free to call me Jim."

Fortunately for Janeway, she had been in enough bizarre situations, had enough experiences that would have made lesser men and women question their sanity, that she was thrown only for a few moments. She recovered quickly from her initial shock, and then said briskly, "I'm quite certain I'm not dreaming."

"How would you know?" asked Kirk. He walked casually around the small quarters, looking disapproving.

"I know because I dream in black and white."

"Perhaps you're only dreaming that you're dreaming in color," he countered. He gestured around himself. "Space may be infinite, but obviously not in here. They couldn't provide you with larger accommodations?"

"I wasn't expecting to share them. Who are you?" she demanded. She felt no need to summon help at that point; she didn't feel as if she were in any immediate danger. Besides, it was a science vessel, not a starship, so it wasn't as if a crack security team was going to come running.

"I'm James T. Kirk." He tilted his head slightly, quizzically. "Are you having short-term memory difficulties? You may want to see somebody about that."

"I know you're supposed to be James T. Kirk. That's who you're presenting yourself as. But obviously you're not."

"Why are you fighting it, Kathryn?" he asked with what he doubtless thought was suavity. He smiled wryly. "You once said you wish you could have teamed up with me. So what's wrong with getting your wish once in a while?"

Her eyes narrowed, her mind racing toward an inevitable conclusion. There was no trace of amusement in her voice. "All right. Drop it."

"Come on, Kathryn," Kirk said wheedlingly. "I was famous for flaunting Starfleet regulations. You know that. Everybody knows that. Picard's mistake wasn't disobeying your direct order to wait for Seven of Nine and then, and only then, seek out the Borg cube that his 'link' to their hive mind had detected. His mistake was consulting you at all. He should have done just what I always did: Send off a brisk message telling you what he was up to, gone off and done it, and then waited for you to tell him that you trusted him to make the right call. Or is that the problem?" He regarded her thoughtfully. "Are you having trust issues, Kathryn? That's it, isn't it. You dislike having to reach into yourself and trust others."

"I," said Janeway through clenched teeth, "am

not about to discuss any of my personality traits, real or imagined, with you . . ." And then she paused and added with a firm flourish, "Q."

Kirk blinked in overblown surprise. "Is that a failed attempt to utter a profanity? I hardly think it's warranted."

"What is it this time, Q? Another civil war under way in your Q Continuum? More problems with your son? Or were you just sitting around in whatever plane it is that you reside and you suddenly thought, 'You know what? It's been ages since I tried to annoy Kathryn Janeway, so I think I'll have a go of it. But maybe, just maybe, if I show up looking like someone else, she'll be stupid enough to fall for it.' Nice try, and it might have worked were I monumentally stupid. So drop the façade. It's not as if you even knew James T. Kirk."

"Don't be so sure of everything you think you know, Kathryn. You see"—Kirk smiled—"even I, who truly *do* know everything, know enough to know what I don't know."

Kirk's form suddenly shifted, and Janeway was fully expecting to see the smug face of the cosmic entity known as Q standing before her. Who else, after all, would it be? Who else would show up out of nowhere, looking like someone who was long dead, and acting in an overly familiar and generally insufferable manner?

So she was understandably startled when she saw something other than what she was expecting.